A native South Carolinian, Wesley Moore III taught English at Porter-Gaud School in Charleston for 34 years before his retirement in 2018. He has published in literary magazines, won several writing awards, and has had a short story and poem anthologized.

In addition, he is a pictorial artist who specializes in narrative photo collage.

Wesley lives with his wife Caroline and stepdaughter Brooks on Folly Beach, South Carolina, the Edge of America. You can check out more of his writing and some of his art on his blog, *You Do Hoodoo?* (wlm3.com).

In memory of Judy Birdsong Moore (1954–2017)

For Caroline

Wesley Moore III

Today, Oh Boy

AUSTIN MACAULEY PUBLISHERS™

LONDON • CAMBRIDGE • NEW YORK • SHARJAH

Ordering Information
Quantity sales: Special discounts are available on quantity purchases by corporations, associations, and others. For details, contact the publisher at the address below.

Publisher's Cataloguing-in-Publication data
Moore III, Wesley
Today, Oh Boy

ISBN 9781685626112 (Paperback)
ISBN 9781685626129 (ePub e-book)

Library of Congress Control Number: 2023900469

www.austinmacauley.com/us

First Published 2023
Austin Macauley Publishers LLC
40 Wall Street, 33rd Floor, Suite 3302
New York, NY 10005
USA

mail-usa@austinmacauley.com
+1(646)5125767

Many thanks to David Boatwright for the cover art.

Bigtime appreciation for those who read the manuscript in its various phases and offered encouragement and/or frank assessments: Sean Scapellato, Robert Fowler, Robin Kellam, Kelly Lynne Schaub, Cintra Wilson, and especially Caroline Tigner Moore for her keen eye, thoroughness, and abiding patience.

First Period

Summerville, South Carolina, Homeroom (8:00–8:05 A.M. Monday 12 October 1970)

A mango-hued, pockmarked bulletin board hangs on a classroom wall of pale lime green concrete blocks, the bulletin board pencil-stabbed and compass point-gouged. Among the graffiti are the names of the star-crossed lovers: Sandy + Tripp. Tragic Tripp, whose body was found last week tangled in blackberry bushes along the banks of the Ashley River, his skull smashed after falling off Bacons Bridge.

S-A-N-D-Y + T-R-I-P-P.

Rusty Boykin, a skinny, freckled redhead sitting on the bulletin board row in Mrs. Laban's homeroom, traces his index finger in the depression of Sandy's name. He supposes it's Tripp's work – the letters inartistic, juvenile. Sandy hasn't been to school since Tripp's death, four class days ago, and now it's Monday, and she's still not here. She should be sitting right in front of Rusty, her honey-colored hair hanging like a curtain to her waist.

Six-foot-two Ollie Wyborn, a newcomer to Summerville, sports round wirerimmed glasses and parts his dark brown hair down the middle. He has compartmentalized Tripp's accident into the "one of those foolish things" category, the accident reinforcing Ollie's cautious approach to life. Right after the tragic news, Ollie overheard Alex Jensen call Tripp's death "natural selection at work," and although recognizing it as a sick joke, Ollie chuckled inwardly because Tripp's death does neatly correspond to Darwin's theory. It surprises Ollie, though, that AJ – as everybody calls Alex – knows enough science to make a witty crack like that. AJ seldom does his homework. You're more likely to catch him reading a contraband magazine like the *National Lampoon* than a textbook. Last month, Mrs. Laban confiscated an issue of the *Lampoon* from AJ that had a cover photo of man holding a gun to a dog's head with the caption, "If you don't buy this magazine, we will kill this dog." Ollie has heard that AJ smokes marijuana, whose active ingredient, THC (tetrahydrocannabinol), negatively affects cognition. To Ollie, smoking marijuana is just as stupid as tumbling off a bridge at night. Well, maybe not quite as stupid.

Unsmiling, Mrs. Laban stands vigilant in front of the room, a science lab/classroom with a sink-equipped black cabinet standing as a barrier between her and what the kids call the blackboard, though it's actually green. The board displays homework assignments written with color-coded chalk in cursive that features economical loops and emphatic exclamation points! Others are milling in: the principal's daughter, Sallie Pushcart; petite, blonde, glassy-eyed Meg Blackthorn; Mama-Cass-sized Althea Anderson; and Josh Silverstein, wired as usual, a manic, metallic grin flashing beneath old-fashioned, black-framed glasses. Mrs. Laban has now donned her Jesus-loves-us smile, her posture dauntingly perfect, as if her spine has been nailed to a straightedge, her blue-tinged silver hair a carefully coiffed construction of Pentecostal perfection.

Rusty, crusted sleep on his lashes and a fresh sprinkling of zits competing with his freckles, dislikes and fears Mrs. Laban. He senses her disapproval of him, of his tangle of unruly red hair and his scruffy blue jean jacket with the rolling paper icon *Mr. Zig Zag* silk-screened on the back. Although Rusty doesn't smoke tobacco, his parents light up like fiends, so the stale scent of secondhand nicotine permeates his clothes. As usual, he didn't open a book last night, so today's Biology II midterm will be a testament to his ability to make intelligent guesses based on esoteric bits of information that somehow penetrated the force field of his daydreams.

AJ slides in just before the bell, rushing to his seat, shirttail halfway untucked, his wavy brown hair mussed, illegally hanging below the collar of his blue oxford shirt. He's leaning forward, Groucho-like, a worn Airway briefcase in his left hand. He, too, hasn't done his homework, having spent last night with Rusty and other miscreants at Will Waring's. Will has dropped out of school and taken up residence in an outbuilding behind his widowed mother's crumbling estate. AJ's no athlete, panting as if he's just competed in the 1970 Pan Am Games' 400-meter dash. Chuckie Cooper, Sallie Pushcart's boyfriend and starting middle linebacker of the Mighty Green Wave, sports closely cropped dirty blonde hair and an eye-singeing red alpaca buttoned up cardigan. He's muttering something about hippies under his breath, but AJ ignores the would-be witticism. As it happens, Chuckie is a frequent subject of AJ's impromptu mockery routines, but homeroom isn't what you would call a friendly audience.

An ear-splitting bell signals the official beginning of school. Mrs. Laban has moved to the right of an anatomical dummy whose plastic flesh-colored "epidermis" has been removed so that its bright, color-coded internal organs are on display. The blue-eyed dummy stares vacantly, smiling into space like an oversized Ken doll. Mrs. Laban and the popular students have dubbed the dummy "George." AJ, on the other hand, refers to it as "The Silent Majority."

As Mrs. Laban peers over her half-moon reading glasses at her roll book, star quarterback Danny Duncan slips in late and slides into his front-row desk, one seat away from where Sandy should be sitting. Dashing Danny looks as if he could be Hollywood heartthrob Troy Donahue's younger brother. With thick, blondish wavy hair and a strong square jaw, he is nothing if not quick. If that had been AJ or Rusty, a detention would have been "awarded," but Mrs. Laban was literally looking the other way. Sitting next to Danny on the front row, Jill Birdsong, a tall, levelheaded, flat-chested, straight-A student, is one of the few girls not enthralled by Danny. She disapproves of Mrs. Laban's playing favorites with him.

Mrs. Laban calls roll, glancing from the name in her gradebook to the corresponding person sitting in his or her assigned seat. Most students say "here" – with a couple of "presents" thrown in – but Danny barks "yo" when his name is called, followed by a friendly chorus of chuckles. Ollie notices that AJ is grinning like a maniac, writing or drawing something in his notebook. Ollie hears own name, the last one called, enunciated in Mrs. Laban's careful Upstate

South Carolina drawl. Rusty notes that Mrs. Laban has skipped Sandy's name; maybe she has inside information on Sandy's mental condition.

Mrs. Laban closes the gradebook and picks up another publication from her desk. She positions herself directly in front of the class. "AJ," she says, "I believe it's your turn to read the devotion." She hands the booklet to Mary Dean, sitting in the first desk of the second row, who passes it to the student behind her, who passes it back to AJ. Although Summerville High is a public school, Mrs. Laban "provides an opportunity" for students to read from *The Weekly Devotional,* a periodical published by the Southern Baptist Convention. The testimonies the students read aloud aren't prayers, but first-person accounts from missionaries, often rendered in gender-inappropriate adolescent voices. Participation is not mandatory, but even Josh Silverstein obliges when the booklet passes from desk to desk down the line to him.

"Yes, Ma'am," AJ says, and as he reads, he alters his accent, drawing out the vowels to make it extra Southern, inflecting the words like a backwoods preacher.

"When Eye-uh was a Seminarian-uh, in the Nineteeeeeen For-ah-ties-uh."

In a battle to stifle his giggles, Josh Silverstein succumbs.

"Alex, that's enough!" Mrs. Laban snaps. "Button it, Josh!" She's fuming. After what the school went through last week, here he is mocking our Lord. "Alex, hand the *Devotional* to Ollie, and you go, son, as fast as your little legs will carry you, straight to Mr. Pushcart's office."

"What for?" AJ asks with mock incredulousness.

"You know, young man. Now get—"

"'Cause I was just trying to bring the devotion to life?"

"You know what you were doing. Being sacrilegious."

"No, Ma'am. I was trying to dramatize the reading to make it more effective. Isn't that better than reading it in a monotone?"

Mrs. Laban's thin mouth is drawn tight, her glowering eyes twin barrels.

"I said, 'Get out!'" she screeches.

Alex Jensen rises scowling.

Mrs. Laban purples.

Jill Birdsong, embarrassed, looks down at her Pre-Cal problems.

Rusty Boykin muses on how wonderful it would be if Mrs. Laban would keel over with a massive stroke and/or coronary—maybe not die but be rendered incapable of administering the impending midterm.

Now that the door has closed behind AJ, the silence is palpable. Mrs. Laban inwardly struggles, trying to control her breathing. Josh has put his head on his desk, and to Althea Anderson, three rows behind, he appears to be violently weeping.

"Ollie," Mrs. Laban manages, "please read."

Ollie pushes his wire rims up on the bridge of his nose and begins. "When I was a seminarian in the late 1940s, I met many men who had served—"

Rinnnnnnnggggggggggggggggggggggggggggggg!

Between Classes (8:05–8:10)

All alone in the main hall, in the posture of someone being led to the gallows, AJ trudges, head lowered, feet shuffling, his eyes focused on his desert boots, each step bringing him closer to a horrible reckoning. He should have known better than to think Mrs. Laban could take a joke.

As the last painful pitch of the bell dies, classroom doors fly open, and AJ is swallowed by the crowd, disappearing into the swarm of chattering students headed for first period, jostling with them right past the milky glass-walled administrative offices. He lifts his eyes and glances forlornly at the office, but discreetly steps aside and pushes open the double glass main doors to freedom. In bright sunshine, he quickens his pace, afraid to turn around. The blond-bricked school behind him is only ten years old, designed to be functional—but it's so soulless, the architecture and landscaping absolutely uninspiring. The carpetweed beneath his desert boots can't keep the sandy dirt from blowing away. A balled-up piece of paper torn from a spiral notebook cartwheels past like a tiny tumbleweed as he sneaks a peek over his right shoulder at the Stars and Stripes flapping in the stiff October breeze.

***

Bent over and groping, too afraid to look, Rusty has plopped into his desk in Mrs. Pinsky's Honors American History class, hoping against hope that he'll feel the comforting bulk of his missing history textbook in the compartment beneath his desk. Rusty has mastered the art of losing things, like notebooks, wallets, birth certificates,

15

report cards, sweaters, baseball cards, his religion, to name only a few.

Jill Birdsong is seated, ready to go. Others from different homerooms file in: Missy Roberts, class president in a plaid polyester pantsuit; Kevin Manigault, one of the few Black students in the entire school system; James Hopper, who takes short steps, his clarinet and books pressed defensively to his chest.

Down past the left turn in the hall in the math wing, Dana Richardson, one of Sandy's closest friends, whispers into Sallie Pushcart's ear.

Rinnnnnnnggggggggggggggggggggggggggggggg…

First Period (8: 10–8:55)

Riiinggggggggggggggggggggggggggggggggggggggggggggg!

AJ can barely hear the distant bell as he closes the door of his VW bug, a white, dented egg on wheels parked among pickup trucks, station wagons, and sedans. He wishes it were a cloudy, rainy, depressing day. Bright sunshine on a Monday morning is the pits, especially when you've just gotten yourself in serious trouble.

He's a careless driver at best, but now he's horribly preoccupied and barely glances to his left as he rolls through the stop sign onto Highway 17-A. Traffic is sparse; pine trees, azaleas, cottages and convenience stores flicker past. The radio is tuned to "the Mighty WTMA," the song, John Lee Hooker meets Billy Graham: Norman Greenbaum's "Spirit in the Sky." He should go straight home and inform his mother or drive to his father's law office, or better yet hang a u-ey and head back to school…but he doesn't.

***

Back in the classroom, Rusty's groping hand encounters in the dark compartment beneath his desk the bulk of a book. He slides it out and upward and onto the grained veneer of the desktop. Whew! There he is, good ol' George Washington on a white horse being rafted across the Delaware. He opens the cover and sees his name among five previous scholars dating all the way back to 1965.

Two rows down, Jill Birdsong has her own book open to the appropriate page, 264. She glances out the window at a basset hound jauntily trotting toward the woods beyond the campus. The bright and sunny day suits Jill's mood. She's not really dreading anything: not the Junior Civitan meeting at Activities Period, not drill team practice after school, not dinner with her blended family, not the Pre-Cal homework problems that will unravel tonight between the blue lines of her loose-leaf notebook paper.

***

Ollie skipped a year of math because he transferred from St. Paul, Minnesota and must take senior Calculus as a junior. Next year as a senior, he'll take Calculus 201 at the College of Charleston—where his father teaches—or that's the plan for now. Unfortunately, because of his unique situation, he can't take Honors American History, so he finds himself in a classroom of somewhat talented but not especially gifted senior South Carolina math students. Not that he considers himself intellectually superior to them; he realizes, quite sensibly, that their preparation has been substandard compared to St. Paul's schools. Colonel Claude Toby Dukenfield, the teacher, has failed to answer so many of Ollie's "why" questions that Ollie's stopped asking them. There's no point in wasting time that could be more productively spent instructing the other students in the basic subject matter. Colonel Dukenfield, patting affectionally his enormously distended paunch, would rather talk about his World War II bombing missions than calculate the trajectories of more mundane objects moving through three-dimensional space. Spittle typically glistens in the right lower corner of his mouth. Unlike his other classmates, Ollie sees this excrescence as unfortunate rather than comical. However, when the spittle amasses to the point of drooling, Ollie averts his eyes.

An only child, Ollie's move from urban St. Paul's to small town South Carolina has been unsettling in more ways than one. Despite the fame of so-called Southern hospitality, Ollie has found many of the natives to be downright unfriendly. He has been dressed down by adults for not saying "sir" and "ma'am" and has had his inflections mocked by people who sound like the characters on *Hee Haw*. He's been called a Yankee, a carpetbagger, and worse. However, as his father has pointed out, it's only for two years, which will pass before he knows it, and the financial and professional benefits of both a full professorship at the College of Charleston and the chance to start a brand-new Asian Studies Program presented an opportunity that his father just couldn't pass up.

***

A mile and a half away, in bed with her twin fluffy white stuffed unicorns, Sandy Welch, her eyes red and swollen, clasps her hands in prayer as she begs Jesus to command her period to come. She had until yesterday been heavily sedated after receiving the horrid news from her mother and Reverend Hale, a fat man whose head is so bald it looks as if it's been polished. The next few days elapsed like a bad dream – the creepy perfumed funeral home, Tripp's devastated parents, his sobbing sister Traci, the Baptist Church with its bright red carpet, stained-glass windows, and peculiar smell. Worst of all, Sandy's beset with the ever-gnawing, horrible fear that deep down inside of her, there's a fetus, or embryo, or whatever you call it. A dead boy's baby!

In the kitchen, wrapped in her pink quilted housecoat, Sandy's mom, forty-five-year-old Liz Welch, quietly mixes her first Bloody Mary of the day. Obviously, Tripp's death is mysterious. A rambunctious boy, a daredevil, but still, what was he doing walking along Bacons Bridge on a school night? Maybe he was drunk, trying to tightrope the rail of the bridge? It's heartbreaking, heartbreaking.

***

Two blocks west on Highway 17A, AJ's white VW zips past the right turn that would take you to Sandy's house. He's on his way to see Will Waring, the high school dropout, who's sound asleep beneath a mural of Jimi Hendrix that he has painted with cordovan shoe polish on the ceiling of an upstairs bedroom in his mother's carriage house. Will's mother, Weeza, indulges her only son, encourages him to cultivate his artistic talent. He has covered the walls and ceilings of his "apartment" with drawings, mostly psychedelia and caricatures influenced by R. Crumb. After an academically disastrous semester at boarding school and a traumatic month at Summerville High, where administrators singled him out and busted him for the slightest infraction, Will has dropped out with his mother's grudging permission. Rusty Boykin has promised Weeza he will do his best to convince Will to go back to school—though Rusty has no intention of doing so. He might as well try to pull an Orpheus, animating Mrs. Waring's moss-draped oaks with the beauty of his three-chord guitar playing. AJ, Will, and Rusty have formed a trio called The Purblind Doomsters, a name Rusty copped from a Thomas Hardy poem. They have yet to land a gig.

Will, who will turn eighteen in April, has other plans. An ominous Selective Service draft lottery looms this summer. He, Rusty, and AJ have plotted a secret escape operation for June, the Big Secret Odyssey (code name BSO). Afterward in the fall, Will intends to decamp to Canada and be a professional artist, silk-screening to earn a living while he works on his great paintings. If his never-failing bad luck holds true and he gets drafted, he would much rather be in Canada working on canvases than dodging hand grenades in Southeast Asia.

***

The Honors History teacher, Mrs. Pinsky, a Navy wife of twenty-six from Cleveland, makes it no secret that she considers teaching in a small, provincial South Carolina public school the anthropological equivalent of a Peace Corps stint in the Sudan. Perched on a stool in a short, tight dress with neon green pop art designs, she offers a contrast to the somber images plastered across her classroom walls: Washington Crossing the Delaware; the Capitol's rotunda; the flag being raised at Iwo Jima; and a grinning, hunched Richard Nixon staring Rich-Little-like from a blue calendar ringed with former chief executives. "So," Mrs. Pinsky says after a sip of her coffee, "who can tell me the losing commander's name at the Second Bull Run—or 'the Second Manassas,' as 'yawl' prefer to call it down here." Except for her mocking twang over "Manassas" and "y'all," her vowels are clipped, slightly nasal, scornful.

"Pope," Rusty barks, hoping that his storehouse of Civil War lore will give the impression that he read last night's assignment.

"And the Southern commander, Mr. Manigault?"

"That would be General Lee, Ma'am."

Connie Pinsky hates to be called 'Ma'am.' However, Kevin is African American and no doubt suffers enough as it is. The Black children in Dorchester County School District #2 have been hand-chosen for integration, like so many Jackie Robinsons: intelligent, middle-class kids willing to take abuse for the chance of a better education. She decides not to chide Kevin, even though she has made it quite clear to *everyone* that she doesn't want to be called 'Ma'am.' She uncrosses her legs then re-crosses them on the opposite side, offering the class a flash of her chunky white thighs and pink panties. All the girls, including Jill Birdsong, dislike her.

***

Around the bend of the hall in Mr. Burke's regular-track Algebra II class, a finger football flies through Danny Duncan's goalpost thumbs. Sallie Pushcart, the principal's daughter, whispers to Susan Smith that she's heard Dana is meeting Sandy this afternoon at three-thirty at Bacons Bridge, the scene of Tripp's accident.

Although it's five minutes into class, Mr. Burke still doesn't have his charges on task. "Come, on, people. Sit down, Josh. Okay, this is gonna be on the test. Don't blame me if you end up flunking and are in a study hall the next six weeks." A recent graduate from the University of Vermont, Quinn Burke, tall with curly black hair, is dressed conservatively in a plain white oxford shirt but wears a way-out-of-style skinny black tie. Althea Anderson, who has a crush on him, is sketching a detailed caricature in her notebook. "C'mon, guys," he whines, "let's get going."

***

Three miles southwest among the upscale homes of the Old Tea Farm subdivision, Liz Welch, Sandy's mother, lights another cigarette after taking a sip of her Bloody Mary disguised as a V-8 in a juice glass. She tunes her console TV to Channel 4, NBC, the *Today Show*. The screen flickers with jungle footage. A helicopter's blades create a virtual hurricane as it descends, blowing the conical straw hat off a small, tanned man whose loose white shirt flaps like a flag in the wind. Liz gets up and switches the station to Channel 5, reruns of *I Love Lucy*.

22

***

Just as Liz Welch changes the channel, across town AJ pulls into Will's driveway, cutting the engine and coasting quietly past what they call the Big House to Will's modest digs in the carriage house out back. Will doesn't lock the door, so AJ slips into "the studio" with its Fender amps and sole microphone stand. Against one wall are a dingy green sofa and a coffee table strewn with magazines and record jackets, but surprisingly no cigarette-choked ashtrays. An old-fashioned loudly ticking clock sits on the mantle of a fireplace that hasn't been used in twenty years. The clock's Roman numerals read twenty minutes after VIII. First period well underway.

Sprawled on the sofa, AJ thinks to himself that running away from school was stupid and will only make matters worse. Ever since he got busted for drinking beer at a school function, his parents have turned into draconian drips, into regular Pat Boones. He'll probably get suspended for three days with failure-ensuring zippos registered on all tests and quizzes administered during his suspension, which he imagines will be spent in his bedroom in solitary confinement with only his schoolbooks to keep him company. If he flunks a class, he can make it up in summer school, but that would disrupt his BSO plans. And he might have been able to talk his way out of it, copping the plea of sincerity, though ever since he got that *National Lampoon* confiscated, his sincerity stock has plummeted. Why, of all people, did Mrs. Laban have to find it? The one with the dog on the cover at that.

***

"What is that you have there, young man?"

She was, of course, frowning, hard-eyed, standing over him at his desk, reeking of some kind of cheap, old-fashioned perfume, and in the early morning light, Alex could see thick, illuminated peach fuzz all over her face, lots of it, like, she almost needed to shave.

"A magazine."

"A magazine hidden in your book?"

"Yes, Ma'am."

"What kind of magazine?"

"A humor magazine."

"Let me see it."

"Please, Ma'am."

"What you mean, 'please, Ma'am?' I said give it here."

When she snatched it from his desk, a subscription card flew out like a doomed person jumping from a burning building. Unfortunately, the magazine flopped open to a cartoon depicting the skeleton of a child wearing a baseball cap trapped in a refrigerator. Flipping through the pages, Mrs. Laban's mouth incrementally opened wider and wider, and she actually said "oh-my-gawd," her taking the Lord's name in vain being as rare as a solar eclipse.

Filth. Sacrilege.

What had been infecting the rest of the nation—promiscuity, rebellion, godlessness, perhaps even communism—had made its insidious way all the way down to South Carolina. To her mind any student carrying such salacious material to school should be permanently expelled. One strike, out. No parole.

Mrs. Laban immediately disliked the looks of Alex's father, a portly lawyer, older than the average father, with a reddish white fringe of hair circling his freckled scalp. Mrs. Laban recognized his type immediately: a pompous blueblood, a Hubert Humphrey voter who enunciates words like an educated Black man, listens to German opera, and favors corduroy blazers with patches on the elbows. In other words, an Episcopalian.

"Why, yes," Mr. Jensen said addressing Principal Pushcart and Mrs. Laban at the parental conference, "I do deem much of the magazine to be in poor taste, though I have to admit I thought that letter to the editor from Marcel Marceau was pretty clever. Did y'all happen to catch that?"

Non-intersecting wavelengths.

Different planets.

Far distant galaxies.

His quip was met with frowns and self-righteous mock-pitying shakes of sage educators' heads as they made their case against his son. Mr. Jensen listened politely for a while, but there was only so much of these jackasses he could stomach, so he retrieved his grandfather's golden watch from his vest pocket, opened it, sighed, and slapped it shut. "All right," he conceded, his affable tone a thing of the past. "I'll see to it that Alex never again brings the *National Lampoon* to school, though I suspect that his bringing a magazine to school is not a violation of any law or stated school policy, though, of course, reading it in class is deserving of punishment. However, in no way can that magazine be construed as pornography as you, Mrs. Laban, erroneously claim. Board of Education v. Zuckerman was a recent case very similar to this. So, I can't see how Alex's punishment should be any different than if he were caught reading a *Mad Magazine* or *Sports Illustrated*. Yes, the magazine strikes me as rather crude, juvenile Juvenalian satire" – (he sardonically smiled at the sound of ju-ju) – "but certainly it is not subversive by any stretch." He added that if *he* were *they*, he'd be more concerned about the school district's own violation of the law, the separation of church and state – shooting a look at Mrs. Laban – and that sixteen years after Brown v. Board of Education, Summerville High School had yet to become fully integrated. He stated in unequivocal terms that any draconian punishment would result in a lawsuit.

***

Willy Monroe has just remembered he has a Spanish quiz later in the day, so he has successfully steered Colonel Dukenfield from how the "squeeze principle" functions in calculus to the high drama of bombing Dresden. The Colonel's stories can be fascinating, and what's more, they provide the resourceful scholar a chance to cop a clandestine peek at those Spanish vocabulary words. That's what Cindy Cauthen, editor-in-chief of the yearbook, is doing. Cindy lives in the same subdivision as Ollie Wyborn and has developed a serious crush. Ollie has picked up on Cindy's undisguised admiration, but his romantic interests lie elsewhere—in the person of Jill Birdsong, though he's been too shy to ask her out. Jill, counter-intuitively, has a crush on Rusty Boykin because she finds him smart and funny, and he reminds her of her redheaded cousins from Tacoma, Georgia. Rusty, of course, is madly, desperately in love with Sandy Welch. Having read *Ivanhoe* over the summer, he's projected the attributes of the novel's heroines Rowena and Rebecca onto wild and reckless Sandy, a character closer to Natalie Wood in a rock-n-roll movie than an avatar of medieval courtly love.

Providing war-movie sound effects, the Colonel rambles on, shuffling before the greenboard, chalk smeared on his pants. Ollie has heard the close cousin of this World War II anecdote before, so he glances ahead in the text, wishing he could get a jump on tonight's homework, which eventually will be assigned in an improvised spray right after the ringing of the bell. When Ollie's mother and father ask him how school's going, he doesn't share his mild disapproval of Colonel Dukenfield. There's something vulnerable about the old man, a legitimate war hero. You can't help but like him, his throwing erasers at miscreants and listening to the NLCS playoffs with a transistor radio and earplugs as he has his students do classwork, which Ollie finds as worthwhile as anything else in the Colonel's class. Ollie looks forward to attending a real calculus course next year. He aspires to attend the Air Force Academy and ultimately to become an astronaut. He realizes he lacks leadership skills, but knowing your weaknesses is the first step in overcoming them. Asking Jill Birdsong to the homecoming dance would be a positive move for overcoming his timidity.

***

As history teacher Mrs. Connie Pinsky slides off her stool, Mike Mulligan purposely drops his pencil to the floor. She reaches up to pull down a screen, the hem of her minidress rising perilously high, stopping just below the panty-carved crescents of her ample rear end. Her unofficial AV aide, Mitch Mitchell, the only boy in the entire school who wears a flat top haircut, is setting up the filmstrip projector in the middle aisle so students can get the best possible visual sense of the carnage engendered by their ancestors' practice of buying and selling human beings. Unbelievably, last week, a student named Rozier Ravenel defended slavery, right in front of Kevin Manigault, claiming that "Neegrahs" (as Rozier pronounced them) were better off under the benevolent despotism of their plantation overlords. Only a couple of students, Rusty Boykin, who enjoys arguing for the sake of arguing, and Cindy Cauthen challenged Rozier's offensive, self-satisfied apostasy. Kevin Manigault sat silent; Jill Birdsong, to Connie's chagrin, kept her views to herself. But Rozier's comment sent Connie into a tizzy. She rose from her desk, paced back and forth in the front of the classroom, waving her arms in exasperation, admonishing Rozier for his unreconstructed blasphemy. Rusty, though a native of Summerville, brought up that slavery-as-a-benevolent-institution was the official position of their "sub-literate" eighth grade text, *South Carolina State History*, a homegrown work that also rationalized the original organization of the Ku Klux Klan as necessary and lauded the exploits of racist governor Pitchfork Ben Tillman, who earned his epithet by running many a hapless Reconstruction Black out of office and eventually out of state. Connie Pinsky hopes that the filmstrip will provide visual proof that indeed, as Sherman famously put it, "War is hell."

She allows Mitch to operate the projector, its beam illuminating mottles of dust that float in the now semi-darkened classroom. The first slide appears unfocused, a crowded Louis Prang lithograph of the Battle of Antietam.

***

As the familiar closing theme of *I Love Lucy* begins and its plush satiny credits scroll up, Liz Welch rises to turn off the television and go check on Sandy, whose acute ears can detect her mother's slippered bunion-bulging feet shuffling across the beige wall-to-wall carpet. Liz gently cracks open the door, a slice of her puffy face appearing in the narrow opening. Mother and daughter share small narrow noses and large green eyes, though Liz's face is creased from days of golfing and lounging poolside. Sandy sits up in bed, clutching one of the unicorns against her uncomfortably tender breasts. Liz pushes fully open the door with her left hand, her right one clutching the juice glass that holds her Bloody Mary.

"Good morning, darling," she says.

"Hi, Mom."

"Sounds like you might feel better."

"I think I do a little."

"Oh darling, I'm so glad to hear that. It's time you got dressed. Maybe think about getting back to school."

"You know," Sandy, says, "I think it might be time."

"Rise up and try to shine," Liz chirps, and takes the last sip of her Bloody Mary, its forlorn lime lying in a smudge of tomato juice and Tabasco. "Maybe we can drive up to Shoney's and have lunch or something."

Sandy's face falls a bit. "I was kinda thinking I might go to Dana's after school. That is, if I could have my car back."

Liz frowns. Her intuition tells her something's up. "Honey, you think you're ready to drive, with the medication and all?"

"I quit taking those pills yesterday," Sandy says. "I flushed them down the toilet."

"Sandy!"

Without meeting her mother's eyes, Sandy gets out of bed, brushes past her, and opens and closes the bathroom door between them.

***

AKA-registered basset hound Hambone Odysseus Macy—Ham for short, the dog that Jill Birdsong spotted outside the history classroom – has dug under the fence of his yard and is following the scent of puppy love, as Daisy, a wirehaired fox terrier, has gone into heat. Droopy eyed and low slung, Hambone wends his way, snuffing the scent that pulls him along like an invisible leash across seas of St. Augustine and centipede, through drainage ditches, across suburban streets and unfenced, junk-strewn backyards. Occasionally he stops to moan the blues. His strange baying startles the toddler standing and clutching the slats of his wooden playpen in the sunroom of a house behind the Welches.

***

Will lies awake now, unaware that AJ's downstairs in the studio. He's staring up at his mural of Jimi, disappointed that the eyes don't look quite right, though the afro is pretty good, along with the five-pointed stars he has buzzing around Hendrix's head, the metaphorical/pictorial depiction of an acid trip.

Will's main concern this morning is that Rusty is going to chicken out on the BSO, their theatrical runaway, even though red-on-the-head himself is the adventure's principal architect. The plan is to build a raft (accomplished) and float down the Ashley River to North Charleston where they will ditch the raft and hop a westbound freight train, a sort of a harebrained amalgam of *Huckleberry Finn* and *On the Road*. Rusty reads voraciously and shares some of his favorite novels' plots with Will. Rusty has glorified the carefree life of Huck and Jim, described their fishing in the moonlight, retold some of their onshore adventures. Also, he has related the exploits of Dean and Sal from *On the Road*, summarized their drug-fueled cross-country odyssey. Rusty's less adept, though, in perceiving the contrast between the mile-wide Mississippi River of Twain's youth and the two-bit Ashley River that runs past Summerville to Charleston. Will has discerned late trepidation in Rusty, who at heart is a rule follower and probably college bound—if he doesn't get drafted, that is.

Rustling comes from below, probably his mother Weeza snooping around, so Will rolls out of bed, pulling on the Lee jeans puddled on the floor. He steals a glance out of his window at his mother's house, large and forlorn beyond an overgrown garden teeming with cats that breed like, well, cats. Will is a handsome boy with a Nordic face, shoulder-length blonde hair, and sensitive blue eyes. His skin glows with health, except for dark smudges beneath those baby blues. Although he shaves every other day, once a week would be sufficient.

He stomps down the steps in his bare feet to find AJ sprawled out on the corduroy couch reading the back of the record liner of Paul Butterfield's *In My Own Dream*. "Uh-oh," Will says.

AJ drops the album on the table.

"Aren't you missing that big midterm today? The one Rusty kept pissing and moaning about last night, bringing everybody down off their cloud." Will's smiling, the last bit expressed in a mocking, exaggerated California surfer voice.

"Oh man." AJ flops his head back against the couch cushions and pushes his hands through his hair. "I'm in deep shit."

Will frowns. "What's up?"

"I got sent to the office, and instead of just going, I split."

Will's concern melts into a smile. "C'mon, man, that ain't feces. That's tapioca pudding."

"My old man is going to kill me."

"Hey, the raft is ready. We could go tonight."

AJ perks up. "It's ready?"

"Yeah, John D. John finished it yesterday."

"Why didn't you say anything last night?"

"BSO stands for Big Secret Odyssey, not Blab Secret Odyssey."

"Get serious, man," AJ says. "That's a summer project. We'd freeze."

"What a wuss. It's only getting down to forty-eight tonight."

"Anyway, you could never talk Rusty into it."

"Ever hear of peer pressure?"

"I'm worried about your grasp of reality, man. You're getting delusional."

Will shakes his head in mock sadness, flicking his head back, flinging blonde locks from his face. He shuffles over to the stereo and hits the turntable's automatic return: a click, arm lift, mechanical shift, slow descent, scratchy crackle, sinister moaning, Black female voices "ooooohhhhhhhing." Side A of the Rolling Stones' album *Let It Bleed*.

Will turns the tuner down from the earsplitting volume of last night's three-beer binge.

"Oh, man," AJ whines. "What am I going to do?"

"Go back to school, wuss. Just go to your next class like nothing's happened."

"I can't do that. That bitch Laban will ask Ol' Man Pushcart what my punishment was. Man, I'm going to get suspended."

"Look, man, you're talking to a high school dropout. Grow some testicles."

"We'd never talk Rusty into going tonight. Plus, we need to get up supplies."

"So what? He can stay if he doesn't want to come along. We got all day to get supplies."

"But it's his idea."

"So what? It's not like it's copyrighted. We can give him an ultimatum. Look, face it. As soon as they realize you're not at school, they're going to call your ol' lady; she'll be calling my ol' lady. We don't have to leave tonight, but we ought to split tonight. Spend the night at Eddie's. Get everything right. Then take off."

"Got any reefer left?"

***

John D. John, the assumed name of a reprobate, lives in Mrs. Fortunak's Boarding House across the tracks on Railroad Avenue. Of an indeterminable age, deeply wrinkled and gray-haired, he favors Army Surplus garb, green National Guard fatigues, topped with a matching Fidel Castro hat. They met him last summer when Will worked at Carolina Home Furnishers and delivered a secondhand television to John D. John's room. After Will and his partner Burt had lugged the 14-inch set up the musty stairs of the boarding house, John D. John offered the boys a beer that Burt (whose mother owns Carolina Home Furnishers) immediately refused, because they couldn't deliver furniture with beer on their breath. John D. John asked them if they knew where he could score a nickel of reefer. Will smiled and shook his head. "No sir," he said slyly. "I wouldn't know anything about anything like that." When the topic turned to pussy, the boys shuffled their feet and said they had to hit the road.

Later, they would encounter John D. John at the poolhall, and one Friday night Rusty overheard John D. John tell Buzz, the poolhall proprietor, that he had once worked as a boat builder. This gave Rusty an idea. He had just finished reading *Huckleberry Finn*, and the novel had blown him away. He envied Huck's and Jim's escape from the deadening monotony of a fixed routine. His imagination could animate in Technicolor the line drawings of Donald McKay sprinkled throughout the *Illustrated Junior Library* edition he had checked out from the Timrod Library. Better yet, he could visualize AJ, Will, and himself living such a life of ease. A float down the Ashley wouldn't last all that long, and not much wilderness was left between Bacons Bridge and Charleston Harbor, but they might spot some gators, coons, foxes, or maybe even bobcats. They'd ditch the raft in North Charleston, hitchhike to the railyards, and hop a westbound boxcar. They'd segue from one century to another, from one set of runaway role models to another. All to the Woodstock soundtrack, Richie Havens banging on bongos, chanting "freedom…freedom!"

***

Besides the thirst that perpetually parches the throat of Colonel Claude Toby Duckenfield, his next dearest enemy is the clock mounted on his classroom wall whose hands seem frozen. The World War II yarn over, he's called the Wyborn boy to the board to try number four of the homework problems, hoping on the one hand that it will take a long time for him to solve the equation, but on the other hand, that the boy *will* solve it and he *will be* able to explain clearly to his fellow students how he unraveled the mystery. He, the Colonel, isn't altogether sure how to work the problem. Of course, the answers appear in the back of the book, but it's math department policy that students show their work. The Colonel flips ahead to check out the next set of problems as the chalk in the Wyborn boy's left hand is tapping against the green slate sounding like a telegrapher sending out an S.O.S.

***

Sandy's in the shower, going through the slow and laborious task of washing her three feet of thick lemon-lightened brown hair. She considers that hair her glory and constantly checks for split ends, or did, before her troubles took on a more draconian aspect, the terrible fight with Tripp, who freaked out when she admitted to him that she had made out with Tradd, the surfer and private-school boy from downtown Charleston, but it is Tripp she really loves, who is dead, probably because of her, and what if she is pregnant? No period in six weeks. If Tripp were alive, she could at least marry him, and as awful as that would be, that's probably what her parents would make her do—but now there's no one to marry. A home for unwed mothers? No way. No, she'd rather kill herself.

Sandy pivots to let the stream of warm water wash the foamy Prell shampoo down across her back onto the small green and blue squares of the shower stall tiles.

She turns off the water to apply conditioner. The stall is so steamy that a peeping Tom would have a hard time checking her out through the fogged-up Plexiglas. After wringing her hair like a towel, she squeezes the tube with her left hand, a generous glop of yellow crème rinse plopping in her right hand. Slowly, carefully starting with her darker roots, she distributes the crème rinse, running her fingers like combs through her hair, like plows, furrowing through the long strands, uprooting several that stick to her arms and hands until she pulls them off and presses them to the shower stall. Now that she can see her hands, she's more methodical, making sure to cover all the vast expanse of her hair, especially the ends. She turns the water back on, but she has been in the shower so long the heat's running out. She turns up the spigot and rinses, the water becoming cooler and cooler, but now her combing fingers glide through the silken strands, so she turns the tap off and opens the shower door, reaching for the nearest towel. She wraps her hair like a turban and reaches for a second towel for drying off before slipping into the blue bathrobe hanging from the hook on the door.

***

Eight minutes away, Ollie computes:

$-1 < \sin x < +1$

$-1 < \sin x < 1$

$x \, x \, x$

$\lim -1 \, x = 0 = \lim 1,$

$x \, x \, x \, x$

$\sin x$

$\lim x = 0.$

When the clicking ceases, the Colonel looks up from his book. "I think that's right," Ollie says in a rather high,

37

strangely inflected Nordic Minnesota accent, his head nodding as he looks over the equations.

The Colonel sprays, Sylvester-the-Cat-like, "Can you explain how you came up with that?" His hands are trembling.

"Well, I sort of 'squeezed' the problem in between two other 'simpler' functions whose limits are easily computable and equal."

"Atta boy, go on." As Ollie holds the class's attention, the Colonel slowly and clandestinely transfers his flask from his book satchel into the right pocket of his frayed tweed sports coat.

***

Jill Birdsong finds the filmstrip presentation a pleasant diversion from Mrs. Pinsky's typical cult-of-personality teaching performances, despite the horrifying Matthew Brady daguerreotypes of Union dead, stiff as boards, their mouths gaping open, frozen, as if they had made eye contact with the Medusa.

Jill's mind wanders to Tripp Trotter, now forever absent, a line perhaps drawn through his name in all his teachers' gradebooks. The day after his death, over the intercom, Principal Pushcart summoned the students to the gym for the announcement. Through a handheld microphone, Mr. Pushcart briefly related the terrible news and then transferred the mic to Mrs. Palmer, the guidance counselor, who explained what emotions the students might encounter. The only dead person Jill has ever seen was her mother, who died of cancer when Jill was nine. After her mother's death, Jill was by her own account "a basket case," getting physically ill before school, crying when her father had to leave town on a business trip, but fortunately, he remarried within a year a wonderful woman named Dee with two sons of her own, and they strove to put the past behind them. In fact, Dee's sons took the Birdsong name as an act of solidarity. As soon as Jill recalls the sight of her dead mother, the filmstrip's last image – "The End" – appears with a blue background. Mitch Mitchell shuts off the projector while someone else flips on the florescent lights, which stutter a second or two before fully engaging.

"Well, Miss Birdsong," Mrs. Pinsky asks, "what's your gut reaction to what you learned from the slide show?"

"Gut reaction? You mean my emotional reaction?"

Pinsky huffs impatiently. "Yes, your gut reaction."

Jill, a very private person, doesn't like attention or to share her feelings.

Tensing, she responds with forced cool indifference. "The loss of human life in such magnitude is certainly sad, but it happened so long ago I can't really say I have an *emotional* reaction."

An expanding look of disapproval slowly sours Mrs. Pinsky's face.

"It's the Founding Fathers' fault," Rusty interjects.

Grateful, Jill looks across the room at "Mr. Boykin," who is wearing a blue service station attendant's shirt with the name "Buddy" stitched in red cursive inside a white oval over the breast pocket.

"Why don't you go ahead and move to Russia and become a communist?" Jackie Geat spits with more than a little venom. Jackie's father and mother belong to the John

Birch Society and play active roles in the burgeoning Republican Party of South Carolina. "Who's ever heard anyone criticize the Founding Fathers? Without them we wouldn't even have a country."

"Come on, Miss Geat," Mrs. Pinsky says, "There's no need to get personal."

"Communist like Jesus, you mean?" Rusty shoots back.

A discernable, collective sound of surprise rustles through the room, a sort of semi-gasp.

"Jesus lived in a commune, didn't He? With the twelve disciples, sharing everything. Well, if he lived in a commune that, by definition, makes him a commune-*ist*. It's indisputable. It's etymology."

"That's sacrilegious," Jackie's practically shouting. She's a pale, slightly plump girl with unfashionably short hair, teased and frosted blonde.

"Well, actually, it's not," Mrs. Pinsky interjects. "Mr. Boykin's right. The economics of the gospel are communistic. In fact, priests in Central and South America preach communism from their pulpits, because they see it as a central tenet of the Gospels. People, the miracle of the loaves and fishes isn't exactly out of Adam Smith! But, Mr. Boykin, what do you mean that you're angry at the Founding Fathers? Elaborate on that if you would."

"It's, like, what you were saying when we were studying the Constitutional Convention. The Founding Fathers copped out on the slavery question, delaying the inevitable, which the Civil War ended up settling in about the worst way imaginable."

As Jackie Geat rolls her eyes, her contact lenses glide in harmony to their orbits. Mrs. Pinsky is probably a communist herself. And Rusty is such a brown noser. *It's like what you were saying.* Plus, Pinsky grades unfairly. If you don't regurgitate her leftist politics on your discussion questions, she takes points off.

"But wait a minute," Missy Roberts, the class president, adds. "If the Founding Fathers hadn't compromised on the slavery issue, the United States wouldn't exist."

"That's right," Jackie barks. "Our debt to the Founding Fathers is huge. Criticizing them is unpatriotic. We are in the middle of a war if anyone hasn't noticed."

***

Althea Anderson, who has yet to kiss a boy, accepts that she'll never be fashionably thin and has embraced her earth mother archetype. Her middle school years proved difficult with "Fatty, Fatty 2 x 4/ Can't get through the bathroom door" ringing in her ears. Althea's mother, Gladys, stands at 5'2" and weighs 180 pounds. Althea looks exactly like her, a genetic clone practically, but, of course, Althea is less conventional. She has waist-long, jet black hair and wears baggy dresses that come down to her ankles. The counterculture has been a refuge for her. Last year, when Will, Rusty, AJ, and Meg were suspended on Moratorium Day for wearing black armbands, she was right there with them, protesting the war, though she got the impression that Rusty and AJ were participating not so much to protest US policies in Vietnam and not so much as a protest against the needless butchery, but more as a gesture of defiance against school. Nevertheless, they welcomed her and have developed a friendship. In fact, she and Meg Blackthorn, a girl originally from California, have become best friends.

Althea enjoys Mr. Burke's math class, not only because of her crush but also because it gives her a chance to do what she loves best, to draw. She and James Hopper, both gifted visual artists, have shared the role of outcast, though his plight, she recognizes, has probably been worse. Because he is effeminate, James has been the butt of incessant cruelty since the first grade, and to Althea, his scapegoating is stupid because James is the most talented kid in the entire school, undoubtedly destined for greatness, if not fame and fortune. Not only is James a talented visual artist, he's also first clarinet in the concert band. However, all Summerville cares about is football. It's like a religion, or better yet, like ancient Rome. Every Friday a raucous pep rally rattles the rafters of the gym, where the entire school assembles to spur the gladiators into an adrenalin-fed frenzy. Talk about stupid. Boys in pads and helmets running into each other, fighting over an inflated pig bladder, or whatever they call it. And the cheerleaders are practically worshipped as goddesses. The entire spectacle smacks of paganism. An invisible light bulb flashes above her head – Ta-da! – she could compose a satirical painting depicting a pep rally as a decadent Roman spectacle, sticking it to the corrupt administration and lemming-like student body. She smiles, displaying perfect, dazzling white teeth.

A finger football plunking her in the back erases her smile, but Althea doesn't bother to turn around or acknowledge the boyish giggling behind her. Meanwhile in 'Nam, she muses, boys about their age are getting blown to bits. What she wouldn't do for a cigarette. The clock reads

8:41. Fifteen more minutes to art, her favorite class. She flips over to a fresh sheet of her pad and sketches Principal Pushcart in a toga. He does, in fact, sport a Caesarean comb-down, his thinning gray hair stretching across the pink patches of his scalp.

***

Principal Pushcart sits in his office reading the sports page of the *News and Courier*, founded in 1803, the South's oldest daily newspaper. John Pushcart is a rabid Clemson fan, orange and purple his tribal colors. He started three years for the Tigers as a tight end in '47, '48, and '49—'48 being the greatest Clemson team in history, going undefeated at 11-0. Football to Principal Pushcart provides a microcosm for the struggle of life where dedication, hard work, and team play combine to create success. He has been unable to sire a son, a great disappointment, which he deems a personal failure given that the husband is responsible for producing the male-determining Y chromosome. Born in 1929, his child-producing days are now numbered. He's having an affair with Sissy Cummins, the attractive, dangerously perky secretary down at the District Office, but she's on the pill, and his own wife Bernice had to have her tubes tied after the birth of Brandy, their second daughter.

John Pushcart doesn't like change, and as far as Clemson football goes, 1970 has been a year of immense change. For one thing, legendary coach Frank Howard has retired. For another, the Tigers have adopted a stupid orange Tiger Paw as their logo after commissioning a PR company to come up with something modern. Even worse, Clemson has lost two consecutive years to the University of South Carolina, their archrivals.

Closer to home, the Green Wave stands undefeated so far this season, led by legendary coach Sam Schabel who has won the state title five times in his eighteen years as head coach. In fact, John Pushcart credits Summerville's strong football tradition as a powerful antidote to the encroaching moral breakdown other schools in the Tri-County area have experienced. Principal Pushcart believes in taking the bull by the horns, so he actively targeted that Waring boy, a charismatic negative leader, nailing him with every minor infraction until he dropped out. Now if he could only drive away the Jensen boy, he believes his iron grip will be assured. Rusty Boykin's a bit of a problem, but he's a follower, not a leader. It's the negative leaders you must look out for. To knock out of the game if you can.

However, now Tripp Trotter's death has thrown everything into chaos. Although no notes have been found, John Bigelow, the chief of police, believes Tripp's death was a suicide, though by an implausible method. After all, Tripp, an avid hunter, owned both a .410 and 20-guage shotgun. Why would he dive headfirst off the bridge in October, hitting a tree stump, caving in his skull? Of course, kids dive off that bridge all the time. But alone? At night? Fully clothed? If there can be any good news in this terrible tragedy, it's that Tripp's death offers a powerful lesson to teenagers who believe they are immortal. Another plus: Tripp's passing seems to have inspired the football team, who dedicated last Friday's game to his memory and played an inspired forty-eight minutes on the gridiron, handily defeating a pretty good Hanahan High squad. Of course,

Sam will miss Tripp at defensive right guard, but that Bosheen boy, though as dumb as a post, filled in remarkably well Friday night.

***

Tiptoeing up the carpeted stairs, Liz Welch hears the reassuring hum of Sandy's hairdryer, so she turns around to mix herself one last Blood Mary before she sets out on her day's errands. She has agreed to allow Sandy to have the car after having talked to her husband, Dave, an executive at the new G.E. plant in Ladson. Dave confiscated Sandy's Mustang after she had gotten inebriated at a party at the Richards's when Dana's parents were out of town. The transition from Croton-on-the-Hudson to Summerville has been a difficult one. Sandy, an only child, was adamant about not wanting to move. Not only did she not want to leave her friends but she also hated giving up the city as well: Broadway plays, ice skating at Rockefeller Center, and rock concerts. However, to Dave and Liz, one of Summerville's main draws is its old-fashioned, smalltown aura, a place where life is slower and temptations fewer. And it seems that Sandy, aided by her undeniable beauty, has fallen in with the right crowd, the jocks and cheerleaders. Better to be experimenting with beer than marijuana. In fact, Sandy recently received from President Nixon a printed note thanking her for signing a nationwide petition (the local effort organized by Jackie Geat) in support of the war, something that Sandy would never have done in New York.

AJ, who takes great pride in his ability to roll joints, runs his tongue over the gummed edge of the rolling papers. He copped the cannabis from a dubious surfer dude from Folly Beach who charged AJ five bucks for three-quarters of a nickel bag. AJ sifts the powdery green herb between his thumb and forefinger, distributing it evenly within the open papers.

To smoke the joint, Will and AJ have removed themselves to the detached junk-filled garage where the finished raft rests upon nine sawhorses. Mother Weeza, in her naivety, would mistake the unmistakable odor of marijuana for cigarette smoke, although they smell nothing alike, and she, like Will, has a virulent hatred for the substance that killed her husband. The weed's harsh, so each of the boys has a hard time holding in the smoke without coughing.

"So, the USS Kerouac's ready," AJ gasps, pointing to the raft.

Will has inhaled two lungsful, so he just nods in assent, smoke issuing from both nostrils.

The raft is 11' x 8' with a plywood lean-to big enough to sleep two. John D. John, a day laborer at Flack-Jones Lumber Company, has "supplied" the materials and labor in exchange for marijuana. AJ, whose family is quite well off, also has thrown money John D. John's way.

"How we gonna get it to the river?" AJ asks.

"My cousin Eddie has a boat trailer at his country house. We can borrow it anytime we want. We'll drive out there and hook it to my van. Come on, man, let's go tonight. You have nothing to lose. Even if we get caught, you won't be in any more trouble than you already are. Like I said, you got nothing to lose, man."

A crash of broken glass startles the boys. One of the unnamed calicos has knocked a jar of nails off the table.

AJ, in mock melodrama, holds his bursting heart. "Oh, my Gawd," he bellows, "O, bladder, don't forsake me now! I think I'm gonna swoon!"

"Hey, man," Will says, unamused, getting back to the matter at hand, "when we finish this joint, let's drive up to the railyards to scope out potential freight-hopping spots. Once it's known you're missing from school, I wouldn't be at all surprised if Pushcart and your folks sic the cops on you."

"I can't drive in this condition," AJ says, taking the joint from Will.

"Yes, you can. Follow me to Eddie's country house, ditch your car there, and I'll drive us up to North Charleston to the railyards. I already have an idea of what might be a good spot. I wonder if we can somehow cop a schedule for freights coming in and out of certain plants."

***

Colonel Dukenfield has charged his minions with two in-class problems using the squeeze principle, explained by Ollie, so he has excused himself, ostensibly to use the restroom. A huge veined bulbous nose dominates his round, puffy, flushed face, though there's still a gleam in his squinty blue eyes, especially when he's talking to a pretty lady. His knees, though, are killing him, along with his corn-riddled toes stuffed into a pair of scuffed black wingtips, the only dress shoes he owns. Once he reaches the faculty men's room, he closes the door and takes out the pewter flask that bears his name and the name of his plane, the Flying Fortress, etched handsomely in ornate, old-fashioned cursive. He sloshes the Jameson's whiskey around before taking a long, hard draw. Carefully, he screws the cap back on and places the flask in the right pocket of his blazer.

Standing before the mirror, he leans closer, staring into his milky, bloodshot eyes. Mechanically, he takes out the mouthwash bottle he carries in his left pocket and pours in a mouthful, sloshing it around his ground-down molars, gargling it across his cigarette-scorched throat. He spews the green, foamy mouthwash into the sink and turns on the tap water to wash it down. Might as well take a leak while he's in here. He shuffles over to the urinal, unzips his pants, and removes the old airman from the stockade so it can do its business. A weak stream of egg yolk urine splashes the porcelain of the urinal as the Colonel, taking his own sweet time, whistles "There's a Tavern in the Town."

***

Heedless of honking horns and squealing brakes, Hambone, awash in clashing odors, zigzags his way past the uric markings of male competitors, past the tempting waft of garbage, past the uninteresting perfume of tea olive, past the acrid tar stench of subdivision street pavers, through the musky mist of cat spray, his nose twitching spasmodically, tuning into the invisible but palpable essence of Daisy's olfactory come-hither. He stops, sits, raises his head, and moans a tortured lament to cottony clouds floating above his head in the blue of the October sky.

***

Connie Pinsky is pointing out tomorrow's assignment, which she has written on the board. She hates to end the class in mid-sentence and doesn't mind the kids chatting for five minutes or so before they ramble off to their next class. This discussion, she believes, has been successful. Rusty and Jackie really got into it. Jackie's an ass, though it's not really her fault. She's just a dutiful *tabula rasa* whose tablets have been filled with parent-generated propaganda. Tomorrow, Connie finishes the Civil War and relishes the chance to dive into Reconstruction. These five minutes also provide a chance to reflect on how she might adapt what she's done for the less-bright students she'll face next period. She reminds herself to make sure Josh Silverstein sits in the front seat right next to her. If that boy's not on speed, then her maiden name isn't Collingswood.

***

If only the Colonel had assigned the homework before he left the classroom, Ollie could have knocked out the problems in no time. Sighing, glancing down at his aviator's watch, Ollie turns to pack his Calculus book in his bookbag. Two minutes remain, time to read over his English essay one more time. Naw, it's already folded, been proofed twice, no need really. Why not plan a strategy for asking Jill

49

to the homecoming dance instead? She'd go with him, his friends Mark and Matt insist, *even if she doesn't want to*. But still, he dreads asking, can't muster the courage to dial the number. He has already decided to address whoever answers with, "Hello, this is Ollie Wyborn. May I speak to Jill, please?" Maybe he should call to chat before he asks her out, or maybe ask her something about school. Maybe ask her about those John Donne poems he's peeked ahead at. They make absolutely no sense to him. Now, that might be not a bad strategy. Yes, that's what he'll do. Donne is tonight's reading assignment. He'll call her after school.

Rinnnnnnngggggggggggggggggggggggggggggggg!!!

Second Period

Mrs. Eula Lynne Laban, who has second period free, waits for Camilla Creel, lost and lonely, dawdling, packing her things. Camilla, a poor girl from Booneshill, wears a thin linen dress with an ill-fitting white sweater draped over her freckled shoulders. "Come on, honey," Eula Lynne Laban says smiling, her foot tapping nervously beneath her desk. "Let's go, honey! Giddy up! I'm on a mission!"

Camilla looks up and reluctantly smiles, her surprisingly weathered sixteen-year-old hand automatically rising to cover a pronounced overbite. She has no memory of her father and lives in an abandoned school bus that has been fitted with a pot-bellied stove. She, her sisters, and mother sleep in the back of the bus on pallets in "rooms" divided by hanging blankets.

Although the bus lacks plumbing, an outhouse and pump-well are outside twenty yards from their "home." Hurricane lamps provide light. No one at school knows the extent of the Creels' crushing poverty, that Camilla walks each morning a half mile through the woods to the bus stop, leaving one school bus to board another. Though not fully aware of her situation, Mrs. Laban senses something's not quite right with Camilla, who waves goodbye as she exits the room, her free hand raking frizzy orange hair.

The halls reverberate with the trooping feet of students: leather boots, sneakers, desert boots, tasseled alligator loafers, work boots, buckled square-toed slip-ons, motorcycle boots, tennis shoes, dirty white bucks, penny loafers, Hushpuppies: squeaking, scuffling, stomping, clomping, gliding along their communal and separate ways.

Eula Lynne figures she just might as well wait until the exodus is over before cruising down to the office to follow up on Alex Jensen. Nothing's sacred to that boy – no, not even the sanctity of human life—if that filthy magazine is any indicator. It's one thing to possess freedom of religion, she'll grant you that, but no one has the right to mock other people's faiths, and that's exactly what that boy was doing. Born with a silver spoon in his mouth. Doesn't bother to even bring his books home from school. She's seen him walking toward the parking lot with not a durn thing in his hand. Eula Lynne's daddy worked two jobs to send her to Teacher's College, her mama took in sewing, and she herself waited tables all during her undergraduate years. You can bet your bottom dollar she doesn't take her education for granted. What she really resents, though, is that air of superiority that practically emanates from the boy, that smug, mocking smirk on his face.

***

Alex's pal, non-smirking Rusty, is at his locker, struggling with the combination so he can ditch his history text and cop his anatomy notes. He's conceived a brilliant idea for an art project: a neo-cubist rendering of the human digestive tract. Miss Turlock will think it's clever, even if she sees right through the ruse. And who knows? The painting could end up being really cool. The embodiment of utilitarianism, you might say. His short stint in art class has demonstrated to him that he has no artistic talent, so he has decided to go the abstract expressionist route where ideas seem as important as artistic facility, if not more so. Now he has his locker open, but he can't find his notes. The bottom of his locker is a heap of loose-leaf pages from various disciplines, a French quiz here (74), an English essay there (A-), a history test below that (98), then a math test (76), and the most recent anatomy test (57). His frenzied search sounds like rats in a wall, rustling, clicking. Ah, there they are, wadded beneath a crumpled *Mad Magazine* in the corner.

***

Mr. Burke, only 22 years old, bounces around the room on his tiptoes like a prizefighter before the bell, shadowboxing in preparation for Round 2. Because he often forgets to take roll, he hadn't noticed that Alex was missing, and even though Josh Silverstein had excitedly dramatized the histrionics of homeroom, the high-decibel din of various conversations prevented Mr. Burke from picking up on Josh's narrative. His next class is Geometry I, the world of measurement and deductive reasoning. It's a little bit less chaotic than Algebra 2, because some of these kids are advanced ninth graders who've skipped a year, not the slack asses he's just dealt with.

Across campus the boys in shop and agriculture pay no heed to the distant bell. Clad in coveralls or in their blue corduroy jackets, the shop boys measure lumber cuts and loosen bolts while the agriculture boys plant shrubbery and learn about insecticides. They cuss and spit Southern-style, talking 'bout *cooter* and *cuttin' ass* and 440 Overhead Busch cams and football. Giving peace a chance ain't up their alley.

Propelled by red-hot vengeful blood, Bobbey Ray Bosheen's heart thrumps like a punching bag. He's one of the shop boys, a claw hammer in his right hand, his oddly spelt Christian name(s) stitched in yellow on the grayish green coveralls along with a Confederate battle flag his sister sewed on the sleeve for him. Bobbey Ray has developed a raw inchoate hatred for hippies, one of them in particular. Red-on-the-head-like-a-dick-on-a-dog. Whap, he pounds a nail. That gotdamn dungaree jacket and that gotdam way of walking what makes his hair bounce up and down, flaunting. Whap. Bobby Ray's been picturing how much fun it would be to give that bitch a barbering. Whap. He ain't positive, but pretty damn sure he seen him riding 'round in a hippie van along with a jig, a jig with an afro big as a basketball. Whap-whap-whap-whap.

Kevin Manigault, the A.M.E. preacher's son, is making his way to pre-Cal, along with Jill Birdsong, Cindy Cauthen, Rozier Ravenel, and the rest of the advanced math group. They all skipped 7th grade math and took Algebra I in the 8th grade, so they're on track to take calculus their senior year—or they could skip math altogether, though none of them will. They're headed to college, maybe an out-of-state college. Jill's been looking at Davidson. Rozier's bound for Sewanee, like every other member of the Ravenel clan dating back over several generations. Kevin is a shoo-in at SC State, though he'd love to go to Duke, so he's been practicing his S.A.T. on the side. He lives in a Black community called Germantown on the edge of Summerville's city limits. His mama teaches third grade at Alston, "the separate but equal school" on the other side of the tracks.

Camilla Creel, on the other hand, divides her classes among business and home economic courses, though Home-Ec is a waste of time because she already knows how to sew and boil a pot of grits (and pluck a chicken and clean a squirrel). Second period for her is typing, something that she dreads because of her slow fingers and bad spelling. She better hurry up, or she's going to be late, and Mrs. Boatwater ain't nearly as nice as Mrs. Laban.

***

The Art Room is in a separate building that also houses an upstairs Band Room. The Studio, as Miss Turlock calls her room, is a large rectangular space with rows of paint-splattered tables and portable metal stools. She has decorated the studio with an eclectic sampling of student art: twisted torsos in clay, charcoal seascape sunrises, an impressive pen and ink rendering of Chartres Cathedral, a pasty-faced Joni-Mitchell-wanna-be self-portrait, and squiggly psychedelic posters. The room exudes a pleasant sense of productive disorder amid the pervasive smell of paint. Becky Turlock has just turned thirty, and though she loves the kids, this year very well might be her last at Summerville High. Maybe she'll relocate to Atlanta, she's not sure, but she would like to live somewhere more progressive.

She takes teaching art seriously and begins class with five minutes of communal instruction. With twelve students, she can take roll visually, and only AJ and Rusty are missing, which might not be coincidental. A minute remains before the bell. She punishes tardiness, because art's as important as any other subject, and students' not being on time is one of a growing collection of pet peeves. As she peeks through the narrow square window of the door, she sees Rusty hurrying with a handful of papers cradled in his arms, and sure enough the wind snatches away one so

RRRRIIIIIIIIIII—

Second Period (9:00–9:45 A.M.)

-IIIIIIINNNNNNNNNNNNGGGGGGGGG!!!

he pirouettes and chases the sheet of paper. It's comical, the taunting wind snatching the sheet of paper just as Rusty reaches for it – again and again. She smiles, picturing Charlie Chaplin in a silent movie.

Inside, the students, perched at their designated stools around various tables, quietly chat with their neighbors.

"Is AJ not here?" Miss Turlock asks.

Althea constructs a rueful smile. "Well, he's at school, but not here." Although born in Summerville, Althea sounds as if she's from the West Coast, her voice a bit affected, somewhat patrician, distinctly hip.

"And?"

"Mrs. Laban booted him to Mr. Pushcart's office."

A small clattering of communal gossip.

Miss Turlock: "Uh-oh."

The door opens, and Rusty flusters in, sweating though it's a crisp 62 degrees outside. "Sorry I'm late," he sighs, clutching the papers like remnants salvaged from a burning house.

Knowing that they're often partners in crime, Becky asks Rusty, "What's the latest on AJ?"

"Dunno," Rusty says innocently, dropping the papers on the table before shedding his blue jean jacket. "But ziss I do know: dey haff wayz of dealing wit peoplez like him."

The class laughs, and Becky herself smiles. She resents the Administration's heavy-handed enmity toward the counterculture, having witnessed Pushcart harassing Will Waring until he quit school, sweet-natured Will, about as dangerous as a Vanilla Coke. Oh, it's okay for the shop boys to pummel each other right here on the school grounds and brandish Confederate flags on their overalls, but Lord forbid an art student don a black armband in a national protest against an immoral war in accordance with his First Amendment right of freedom of expression. No, that just won't do.

***

Will and AJ haven't made much progress in their mission, though they have washed their faces and gargled with Listerine and anointed themselves with copious splashes of Old Spice to mask the smell of cannabis, producing a chokingly sweet medicinal odor that might raise a red flag to a less clueless mother.

Will has convinced AJ to at least follow him to his cousin Eddie's country place; however, AJ agreed only under the condition that they get a bite of something from the Big House before they set off. Will's own Depression-retro kitchen offers nothing more than an unopened can of Vienna sausages and a half-open sleeve of saltine crackers whose consistency AJ likens to King Tut's toes. This delay, AJ reasons, will allow him to descend a rung or two on the ladder of his buzz and make piloting the Bug less dangerous. On the positive side, getting high has succeeded in exiling his current troubles to that far distant territory on the frontier of his consciousness where thoughts of the upcoming science project have been safely stowed in an impenetrable X-ray proof mental box.

***

Dana Richards, Sandy's best friend, fidgets in Mrs. Campbell's American Literature class. Mrs. Campbell, a no-nonsense, sometimes sarcastic University of Georgia grad, married into a wealthy Old Summerville family and resides in a roomy 1880 clapboard house on Carolina Avenue that features an impressive veranda and a yard brimming with camellias, azaleas, and gardenias.

Dana has read the note from Sandy multiple times, and she's dying to read it again but fears that Mrs. Campbell, who walks up and down the aisles when she teaches, could catch her, confiscate it, and oh-my-god that would be—

She doesn't even want to think about it.

The note was delivered to Dana by that Porter-Gaud boy Sandy had gone out with, a boy who talks with one of those adorable old-fashioned Charleston brogues. Sandy, herself talking really slowly, called Dana yesterday evening to set up the rendezvous. On his way to a college visit, the Porter-Gaud boy—she thinks his name is Thad—met her at the 7-11 right across from campus, a madhouse before school, the last safe place to have a smoke before the monotony of the day begins its slow crawl. Just as Sandy said he would, Thad pulled up in a chocolate-colored Triumph Spitfire. Without bothering to get out of the car, he reached up and handed her the note, and with a nod of the head, sped off, laying a bit of rubber for the provincials to enjoy.

Dana stuffed the envelope in her crocheted purse and bummed a ride with Steve Murray across the highway into the underclassman parking lot. She was dying to read the note, feeling privileged and curious and a little bit scared. Because she's best friends with Sandy, Tripp's death has been traumatic. Being best friends with Sandy isn't like being best friends with, say, Amy, like she used to be, because Sandy doesn't confide all that much. Sandy, unlike Amy, doesn't tell you everything, like what's it's like to kiss so-and-so or how she sometimes hears her parents doing it. Dana suspected that something's not quite right about Sandy even before Tripp went and fell off that bridge—and she has her suspicions—so waiting to read that note in private was excruciating for her.

Mrs. Campbell is droning on about Herman Melville and Nathanial Hawthorne, *dissenters*, she calls them, *anti-transcendentalists*, but Dana couldn't care less about what people thought in 18-whatever. The very word *transcendentalism* irks her. Mrs. Campbell's explanation of whatever it is supposed to mean was about as easy to grasp as an irrational co-sine cubed.

The tone of Sandy's note has Dana feeling really uneasy. She practically has it memorized:

Dear Dana. I know this is short notice but I can't risk saying all this on the phone. Could you please, please meet me tomorrow at 3:30 at the tree at Bacons Bridge? Since I've moved here you have been my very best friend. It's you I want to say goodbye to. To be my messenger. My life sucks. More than you can guess. Would you do this as one last favor? And please don't tell another living soul about this note. You're the only one I can trust, and I know you would never betray me.

Love ya,
Sandy

From the time Dana first set eyes on Sandy, she knew that she wanted to be friends, but being best friends is more than she could ever have imagined. Although friendly with the in-crowd of Danny Duncan and Coo Kitchens, Dana was merely on the periphery of true popularity. She immediately recognized Sandy as someone special; not only was she beautiful but also sophisticated. She told Dana about the time she spotted Dick and Liz in person at a hotel in L.A. and about seeing *Hair* on Broadway. Sandy has experienced glamor firsthand, lived a lifestyle that Dana had only read about in *Cosmopolitan* and *Covergirl*. Dana would never want to betray Sandy, but this note has her scared. It sounds like Sandy's planning something. Something bad. Like running away. Or worse. *One last favor.* Maybe she ought to tell someone, maybe even an adult. In a moment of weakness, she blabbed to Sallie Pushcart she was meeting with Sandy, but she didn't say where or when. Or did she? She can't remember. It's almost like she's losing her mind.

"Dana?" Mrs. Campbell's standing right next to her.

"Yes, Ma'am?"

"Dana, have you been listening?"

Dana's big brown eyes immediately tear up. "No, Ma'am. I'm sorry. I just can't quit thinking about Sandy and Tripp."

At this, she puts her head down on her desk and begins to sob.

***

"Is anyone in there with Paul," Eula Lynne asks the receptionist Mary Kay Cartwright, a twenty-five-year-old bleached blonde chomping on a wad of gum. The door's closed, adorned with a handsome brass sign that says Principal Pushcart, a Christmas gift from his wife Bernice.

"No, Ma'am," Mary Kay says. "He's in there by himself."

"So, Alex Jensen isn't in there?"

"No, Ma'am."

"Do you know what time Alex left?"

Mary Kay looks puzzled. "No, Ma'am. I never saw Alex go in, and I've been sitting right here all morning."

Mrs. Laban's thin lips turn downward into a creased frown as she walks over to Pushcart's door and delivers three crisp knocks with her right hand, ringless and blue-veined.

"Yes," Mr. Pushcart says behind the wooden door, which is locked.

"Paul, it's Eula Lynne. I need to talk to you about Alex Jensen." Paul Pushcart, a *Sports Illustrated* in his hand, begins straightening his desk, stashing the magazine in a drawer. He respects and in a sense fears Eula Lynne, an incarnation of his biblically based superego – a forever frowning Sunday school teacher clad in a white robe, the offspring of John Bunyan and Carrie Nation, an avatar of righteousness, the epitome of godliness.

"One moment, please, Eula Lynne. I'll be right with you."

Mary Kay looks down at Mrs. Laban's tapping foot and hopes that when she gets old her ankles will retain their shape rather than shafting down log-like into hideous blue shoes that – now that Mary Kay thinks of it – sort of do match Mrs. Laban's hair.

A slight clicking precedes the opening of the door as Paul Pushcart gallantly ushers Eula Lynne in with the sweep of his arm. The door closes behind them, and Mary Kay returns to her task of procuring substitutes for tomorrow's classes. Last week was the week from hell with the funeral and all, so she hopes that maybe things will calm down and the weekend will come quickly.

***

In Spanish 3, Ollie dutifully transcribes the overly annunciated Spanish spewing from Señora Garbowski's reel-to-reel tape recorder. Primary colors dominate a room decorated with bullfight and travel posters. In the corner hangs a piñata that the senior class will smash on *Cinco de Mayo*, a tradition Señora started last year, her first year at Summerville High. Like Connie, she is a Navy wife.

From the tape recorder, masculine and feminine voices take turns, reading the passages like radio actors:

Nada sabemos del nacimiento de Don Quijote, nada de su infanciay juventud, ni de cómo se fraguara el ánimo del Caballero de la Fe, del que nos hace con su locura cuerdos.

Spanish comes easily to Ollie. He's always been good at grammar in general, and in many ways, Spanish is much easier than English. Even though Summerville's peculiar grading scale is draconian compared to St. Paul's ten-point scale, he has made an A on every assessment in Spanish, that is, never below a 95. The fact that different schools employ different scales unsettles him because he worries that different frames-of-reference might distort students' performances in the eyes of college admissions officers. For example, his stellar 93 average in St. Paul's Honors Pre-Cal last year would be a B+ on a Summerville transcript, yet last year's pre-calculus course certainly posed much more of a challenge than Colonel Dukenfield's Honors calculus. Here Ollie maintains a perfect 100 average. Of course, that's what the S.A.T. is all about, leveling the playing field.

Nada sabemos de sus padres, linaje y abolengo, ni de cómo hubieran ido asentándosele en el espíritu las visiones de la asentada llanura manchega en que solía cazar; nada sabemos de la obra que hiciese en su alma la contemplación de los trigales salpicados de amapolas y clavellinas; nada sabemos de sus mocedades.

Tonight's homework is to finish translating these passages. Unfortunately, some students cheat by copying each other's homework. Thank goodness the school lacks an official honor code. Not long after Ollie's transfer to Summerville High, Danny Duncan asked to borrow Ollie's homework so he could copy it. Ollie looked Danny squarely in the eye and said, "No, Danny. I can't do that." Danny, used to getting his way, stared for a second, but then turned with a sneer, but that was the end of it. No name-calling. No recriminations. If there had been an honor code, however, Ollie would have been morally obliged to inform the honor council of Danny's infraction. Of course, it would have been his word against Danny's, and if there were any chance that an honor violation would bench Danny, Danny would be acquitted. Ollie, no doubt, would suffer social ostracization, adolescents being notorious for their herd mentality. In this case, Ollie would rather forgo the Pyrrhic victory of doing the right thing and avoid scapegoating. If only they had a lacrosse team down here, but they don't. Even baseball, the national pastime, isn't all that popular in

Summerville. It's 90% football and maybe ten percent basketball with a dash of wrestling.

Despite the treatment he's encountered since transferring from the North, Ollie has refrained from criticizing the "folkways of others," because he recognizes that all cultures possess eccentricities. It does surprise him, though, how often the Civil War comes up as a topic of conversation, especially since World War II has had a more immediate effect on current history with the partitioning of the Soviet Bloc and the dividing of Germany. And what about Korea and Viet Nam? The spread of communism? It seems to Ollie that getting over the Civil War might be an important first step in making progress down here. Certainly, as far as race relations go, many people in Summerville are "backward." The waiting rooms in doctors' offices are segregated, and he's heard that epithet that rhymes with trigger a lot. The official polite word is "colored" because people consider "Negro," the word that news anchors use, a Northern word.

"Nunca busques pájaros de este año en los nidos del ultimo."

***

Across campus, Rusty is sketching the rudiments of the utilitarian masterpiece he has tentatively entitled *Progress through the guts of a Beggar.*

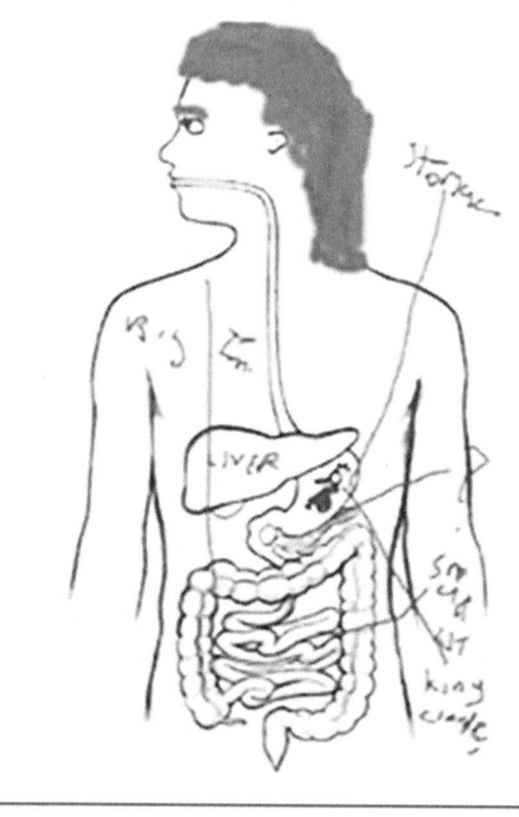

Althea is sitting next to James Hopper, the best-dressed boy on campus, who today sports a black silk shirt, black chino trousers, an authentic black alligator belt, and matching alligator shoes. Copying an old postcard, he's sketching a remarkably precise and detailed illustration of the Old Custom House in downtown Charleston. James has known what he wants to do ever since he can remember. Architecture, of course, is the most enduring of all the arts, and you don't have to go the starving artist route. He's the only child in a divorced family, a rarity in Summerville, and his mother spares no expense to make her son as happy as she can. James's father, whom he rarely sees, sells real estate in Charlotte and has wed a bimbo named Patsy whom James detests.

Althea, who recently discovered Carl Jung's psychoanalytical theories, is conceptualizing her satiric rendering of a Friday pep rally, piloting the spacecraft imagination through the constellation of her collective unconscious, seeking images from the Great Memory, ancient corollary embodiments of contemporary evil.

A loud electronic crackling derails her thoughts. The red light of the intercom has flashed on. Never a good sign. Every class has one, a rectangular speaker box mounted somewhere on the wall. Another crackle.

Speakerbox: (*crackle*) Miss Turlock, Principal Pushcart. Is Alex Jensen in your class?

Miss Turlock: (*looking up at the intercom, addressing it as if a person*) No sir. It was my understanding that he was there with you.

Speakerbox: Who told you that?

Miss Turlock: Althea Anderson.

Speakerbox: By any chance is Rusty Boykin in your class?

Miss Turlock (*still looking up, still addressing the intercom*): Yes sir. He's sitting right here working on a drawing.

Speakerbox: Send him to me. Stat!

Miss Turlock: Yes sir.

Speakerbox: (*crackle*)

All pencils, brushes, kneading hands have halted. Rusty's on his feet, a look of panic stamped on his face. James Hopper glances at Althea, who frowns. Rusty casts a rueful look at his crude rendering of the digestive tract lying next to his open Biology II notebook with its hurried, smudged, barely decipherable and misspelled anatomical terms. He looks up and encounters Miss Turlock's sympathetic, blunt, open features.

"Run along, Rusty. You can leave your things here for now."

"Okay," he says, oblivious to the students' staring faces, oblivious to the clay torsos, oblivious to the smell of paint, oblivious to the splattered tile, oblivious to the silence. He's pushing open the door and stepping into the cool autumn air, oblivious to the yellow disc of morning sun suspended above distant loblolly pines. He's deep inside the auditory darkness of a cave of dread where echoing voices catalog his various crimes and misdemeanors: smoking marijuana; drinking beer; mocking (though behind their backs) administrators, teachers, students, the Mighty Green Wave, Congressmen, Senators, Vice Presidents, Presidents, television shows, movies, Judeo-Christian Deities; purchasing and hiding Playboy magazines for use as visual aids in acts of self-pollution; masterminding a high stakes scheme to run away from home; receiving stolen goods in accordance with the above-mentioned scheme; not living up to his potential.

As an elementary student, if he had been called to the office, Rusty might have feared that someone in his family had died or, on the plus side, that he was being called to receive an award, but his name in conjunction with the initials AJ can only mean trouble. He's forgotten his signature walk, the freak flag flop, and leans forward, head down, oblivious to the pebbly pavement beneath his high-top Converse All-Stars. In the thin cavity of his chest, his heart pounds like timpani as he reaches for the cold handle of the outer double doors. The hall is empty, the only sound the clacking of heels, out of sight, dopplering into the distance. His hand shaking, he grips the handle of the glass doors of the administrative offices, pulling outward.

In the bright florescent light of the outer administrative office, he recognizes immediately that the employees are in an everyday mode. No one has died. No uniformed policeman with badge, billy club, and handcuffs glowers in the corner waiting for him. He clears his dry throat and approaches Miss Cartwright sitting at a desk next to Principal Pushcart's door. As he nears her desk, a tiny pink bubble puffs out from her lips, then pops.

"Mizz Cartwright," he says, his voice unsteady, "I think Principal Pushcart wants to see me."

"Now that's an interesting shirt," she says coyly, snapping the gum. "Where'd you get that?" She's dressed in a yellow alpaca V-neck sweater and a kelly green skirt, the official school colors.

Rusty had forgotten all about his shirt, a new acquisition, the top half of a service station uniform with the name "Buddy" stitched in an oval on its breast, certain to exacerbate whatever vitriol's brewing in Pushcart. Rusty realizes he's left his Mr. Zig Zag denim jacket back in the art room, which is probably a good thing.

"Uh, I got it from Buddy."

"Good ol' Buddy," she says smiling. "Mr. Pushcart and Mrs. Laban are expecting you."

She gets up, knocks, and cracks open the door. "Rusty Boykin is here," she says into the crack.

The muffled bark of a drill sergeant.

"Go on in," she says.

The door creaks open squeakily, like a coffin lid in a Christopher Lee movie. Sitting, leaning forward with his palms down on the surface of his desk, Principal Pushcart looks as if he might be on the verge of doing a hundred or so push-ups. Sitting across from him, looking over her shoulder, a frowning Mrs. Laban pumps her crossed legs like crazy.

"Yes, Sir?"

"Have a seat, son."

There is an empty chair next to Mrs. Laban, a wooden chair, upholstered in some sort of dark green leather-like synthetic something-or-other, the kind of fabric (maybe fabric) that sticks to the back of your thighs when you're wearing shorts in the summer. Principal Pushcart removes his right palm from the desk like some gangster in an old movie and positions it palm-up, then sweeps it in a downward motion toward the chair. Across his scalp strands of brownish gray flimsily stretch in a failed attempt to hide his encroaching baldness. Rusty, dropping into the chair, sighs audibly in tune with the upholstery, which also sighs.

"Now, Blanton," he says, using Rusty's Christian name. "I want you to promise to tell me the truth." His intonation isn't all that unfriendly.

"Yes sir," Rusty says automatically. He's a terribly inept liar anyway.

"You know," Pushcart says, "that Alex Jensen was dismissed from homeroom to come to my office."

This is an easy one. "Yes sir, I was in homeroom this morning."

"Tell me. What did you think of the events of this morning?"

"Think, sir? I'm not sure I thought anything."

"You didn't think it was funny?"

"I wasn't paying all that much attention. I was sort of preoccupied. I have this really big Anatomy test today." He looks over at Mrs. Laban for encouragement, but her features have hardened into a Madame Tussaud's mask of unalterable unhappiness: Lucretia Borgia displeased with the consistency of her soft-boiled egg.

"Did you know that AJ hadn't come to the office?"

"No, sir. Not till the announcement over the intercom."

"Any idea where he's at?"

Rusty successfully stifles the impulse to answer, "Behind the preposition?"

"I dunno," he says instead. "Home, I'd guess. His daddy's office maybe. I dunno."

Pushcart can see the little son-of-a-bitch is telling the truth. "Son," he says, "are you aware that you're out of dress code?"

"It wouldn't surprise me. I guess my hair might be."

"Where's your pride, son?"

Rusty doesn't begin to know how to answer this. A trick question? Of course, he possesses pride, that doom-laden quality that they talk about in English class every year, the moral failing that drives Antigone to break the burial edict,

Ahab to pursue the great white whale, and Macbeth to go all Charlie Manson on his kinsman Duncan.

"I dunno, sir," he says. "You know Alexander Pope called pride 'the never-failing vice of fools?'"

As soon as the words are out of his mouth, he wants them back.

"What?"

"Nothing."

"What did you say?"

"I meant sometimes pride can be a bad thing, so I was hesitant to admit I had some."

"Well, *Mr. Philosopher*, I'm sending you home to get a haircut and to change that shirt. The dress code is rules, son. Not suggestions. Rules. When you look presentable, you come back here to report to me before you resume your education here at Summerville High. Consider it a suspension. Zeroes on all work missed."

"Yes, sir," Rusty says.

"I suggest you hurry."

"Yes, sir."

When he's out the door, Paul looks over at Eula Lynne and asks, "What period is his anatomy test?"

"Fourth."

"Well, then," he chuckles. "I wish him God's speed."

"That secretary of yours is almost as bad as the kids. Out there chewing gum. I don't know about that, Paul. It sets a bad example."

***

Sandy has the window of her Mustang cracked to vent streaming cigarette smoke. She leans forward to turn down the radio, which is blaring an ad for a mobile home dealership – "LOWCOUNTRY MOBILE HOMES!" Despite her desperation, getting out of the house feels liberating. Trees zip past in bright sunshine as she savors the taste of golden-brown tobacco, the tip or her freshly lit Marlboro glowing orange. As if on autopilot, she's headed for school, not knowing what she's going to do when she gets there, probably just drive past, glance at it, a big unfriendly brick fortress, cars lined up in the parking lot.

***

Mrs. Green, a no-nonsense Lowcountry native, explains how to solve a problem on the board while her charges, sitting up straight, follow along. There's not a weak student in the class, though, of course, some are more talented than others. Rozier Ravenel is lazy but as smart as a whip. Kevin Manigault occasionally has trouble picking up on a new concept but keeps at it until he masters it, and the rest, they're topnotch, Jill Birdsong, Cindy Cauthen, the Murray boy. Jeannie Green serves as one of the eleventh-grade class sponsors in charge of the upcoming homecoming dance, which is only two weeks away. Sandy serves on the homecoming committee, but, of course, hasn't been at school for three days. Sandy is responsible for finding and booking a band—she'd been negotiating with some downtown Charleston group—so Sandy's absence makes Jeanne nervous. She likes her t's crossed, her quadratic equations factored, her fingernails polished.

"Let's see if we can do one ourselves, class. Try number 3."

Jeanne glances out of her window to see Rusty Boykin walking rapidly across the quad. She's known the Boykins her whole life, fun-loving folks, especially the mama, Ginny, a nurse. Mr. Boykin flies airplanes for a hobby. She can't remember what his real job is. Something to do with electronics. She's heard recently his business was in some sort of turmoil. A lawsuit or something. She sees Rusty suddenly turn around and head back even faster in the direction he was coming from. Turning from the window, Jeannie notices that Cindy has her hand up and moves over to her desk.

***

For whatever reason, Ollie has never cared about Spanish culture – sombreros and bullfights don't interest him in the least. Summerville offers only French and Spanish, not even Latin, which all students took in the seventh and eighth grades at St. Paul's. Spanish seemed to Ollie a more utilitarian option than French when it was time to choose a high school world language. People speak Spanish in Mexico, all of Latin America, and, of course, in Spain itself. French, though it sounds sophisticated, isn't spoken by that many people around the world anymore. Its heyday as the West's diplomatic language long ago receded into the yellowing annals of the past. Luckily, Spanish is a romance language, so his Latin has helped enormously with vocabulary.

Students have started translating the dictation with open books and pocket Spanish dictionaries. Although Ollie's halfway through the first paragraph, the idea of inviting Jill Birdsong to the Homecoming Dance is tapping on the window of his consciousness, distracting him from his translation. Even if he's successful in enticing Jill to accompany him to Homecoming, Ollie has a problem: he has no idea how to dance. He wishes he had an older sister to teach him the trivial yet important social graces of adolescence, dancing being not an insignificant one. An older sister would offer at the very least an objective correlative for feminine emotions, or more ideally, directly instruct him, explain to him what girls like, what behavioral strategies work with them. Of course, he understands the basic idea of modern dance: primitive music plays, you move your body in an uninhibited manner guided by the structure of the song, yet these movements should fall into some sort of pattern, because if the movements were completely random, you wouldn't have art, of which dance is a genre. Without repetition, you would merely have a series of disconnected, spasmodic movements unpleasing to the eye.

Last night, in the model airplane museum of his bedroom, Ollie tuned his clock radio to WTMA and practiced dancing in front of the mirror. He felt like a complete fool, looked like a complete fool, but he can't very well ask Jill to the dance and then not ask her to dance. Of course, there are slow dances, which amount to little more than swaying rhythmic embraces. In fact, he enjoyed the ones he experienced with Cindy Cauthen, even though he's not attracted to her. At the back-to-school dance, Cindy broke the time-honored patriarchal tradition of the boy asking the girl for the pleasure. As he, Mark, and Matt leaned against the brown brick wall of the gym, Cindy came up to Ollie and said, "I request the favor of the next dance," which thankfully was a slow one, a whiny song with the singer irrationally wondering why the sun continues to shine and the sea rushes to the shore after his girlfriend has dumped him.

Because Cindy's only 5'2", Ollie had to lean and stoop; otherwise, her large bosoms would have pressed against his stomach rather than his chest, though they may as well have been a pair of wooden croquet balls beneath whatever unforgiving brassiere she was wearing. Nevertheless, the idea of her mammilla touching his chest was pleasing, and he danced two more slow ones with her before the lights went up in the gym and he walked alone to the carpool line to wait for his mother to pick him up.

***

In the kitchen of the Big House, Will's mother Weeza has prepared an old-fashioned Southern breakfast of bacon, scrambled eggs, grits, and buttered toast. Will and AJ look sort of groggy, but she doesn't associate those lazy, glazed eyes with any of the well-publicized warning signs of marijuana use. Though tempted, she has decided not to embarrass the boys by mentioning that over-application of cologne can be, as the magazines say, a "turn-off."

Sitting across from AJ at the kitchen table, Will is in a good mood, savoring the aroma of sizzling bacon, appreciating the sound of clattering dishes. Glancing outside the kitchen window, he sees orange leaves fluttering from branches of a sugar maple, the detached leaves spinning like war planes crashing to earth. He turns his attention to the plate Weeza has just placed before him. Dipping a forkful of scrambled eggs into his grits, he waits a sec for the pat of butter to melt. He's smiling, nodding his head, thinking "yes!"

Will believes the phenomenon of life in and of itself should be enough to make a person happy. He can't relate to AJ's and Rusty's reel-to-reel anxiety about so many petty things that ultimately add up to zilch. Will suspects that despite their rebel poses, Rusty and AJ have been, to quote Bob Dylan, "bent out of shape by society's pliers." In other words, society has fooled them into thinking that if they don't jump through its hoops, what society claims is going to happen to them, will happen to them. They lack, in his opinion, the so-called courage of their convictions. Will doesn't have to squander time memorizing the various bones of the human body. He doesn't need to set an alarm each night. He wakes up when his body tells him to wake up. The fashion dictates of polyester-clad fat farts like Mr. Pushcart don't apply to him – he's free. Will believes that becoming society's trained seal profits the circus master, not the seal or the fat lady or the midgets or the clowns.

Okay, let's say you did successfully memorize all the bones of the body and made a 100 on the test, how long would you retain those facts? No way you'd remember them even a year later. In the eighth grade, Will spent hours memorizing the names of all 48 counties of South Carolina. He can still remember a few of them, ones named after cigarettes like Marlboro County; and the Tri-County area counties, Charleston, Dorchester, and Berkeley; but those Indian-sounding ones, like *Itchykitzchywannawanna,* forget it. He could have used that time he wasted memorizing the names of counties more productively, learning something that would stick in his brain forever. If the class had driven up to Marlboro County on a field trip and he could have visited tobacco barns and smelled the cow shit, he'd forever remember that Marlboro County raises tobacco and livestock. And, hey, if you ever need to know the name of a bone, the official name for the collarbone, say, you can look it up. He has argued about his theories of education with Rusty, who claims the process of memorization is like calisthenics for the brain, which sounds ridiculous.

Will's mind wanders to the future, to the Big Secret Odyssey. He's imagining the journey, picturing himself lying on his back and looking up at stars overhead as their raft floats past the old plantations, Middleton, Magnolia, and Drayton Hall. He looks forward to the philosophizing that inevitably accompanies star gazing. He enjoys deep talks with Rusty and AJ because they're smart and funny, even if they do on occasion act like imposters, full of big talk, but carrying tiny little toothpicks, as Teddy Roosevelt or one of those other bushy-mustached presidents sort of said in the opposite way.

While Will has been daydreaming and tuning out his mother, Weeza has been quizzing AJ about his dismissal from school, essentially perp-walking his thoughts right out of lotus land into the dingy confines of a Raskolnikovian closet. During their conversation, Mrs. Waring commiserated with Alex and suggested he call his mother or return to school, but no way she's going to stick her nose too far in somebody else's business. Even though she suspects most of the town think of her as an overly permissive woman who lets her son run riot over her, she doesn't care what they think. She has faith in God, the Episcopalian God who has evolved throughout the centuries from that B.C. Brute of the Old Testament into a tolerant gentleman in a three-piece vested suit, Gregory Peck-as-Atticus-Finch. She believes her God prefers the well intentioned to the righteous, who need, if the truth be known, to tone it down a tad.

***

Jill Birdsong enjoys Mrs. Greene's teaching style. She's stricter than other teachers but is nevertheless friendly, doesn't play favorites, treats everybody exactly the same. Mrs. Greene conveys the material clearly and briskly, though not impatiently. Jill herself is a very patient person. Despite the personal tragedies that darkened her pre-blended families—her mama's death by cancer, stepmother Dee's husband's death by a sudden heart attack—Dee and John Birdsong's home is essentially harmonious and wholesome. She and her sister Ruthie and her two stepbrothers all get along well, especially now that Ruthie and Blazes (her older stepbrother's nickname) have gone off to college, Ruthie to Presbyterian College in Union, South Carolina, and Blazes to Florida State at Tallahassee. Generally, Jill lets other people have their way and doesn't resent it; however, if she feels taken advantage of, she argues her case and argues it well—syllogistically with supporting examples—and so she almost invariably wins.

She knows she's not the Belle of the Ball but wouldn't want to be. In fact, she rarely raises her hand and only if no one else knows the answer and the teacher's getting mad.

Jill does have a hidden personality trait, one that few, if any, recognize. Despite her support for President Nixon, her participation in tons of activities, including the Junior Civitan Club and Young Life, Jill at heart is an ironist. She's silently sarcastic, quickly recognizes the incongruities of the world in which she lives. She possesses—though she certainly wouldn't put it this way—a hypersensitive bullshit meter.

With academics and extracurriculars and family (the Birdsongs eat dinner each evening as a unit even if John must return to his office in tax season), her life is full, and she spends her spare time with her best friends since grade school, Kathi, Nanci and Patti. All three of them belong to Young Life, a Christian organization for teens. Jill has gone on a date or two with one or another of her Young Life buddies, Bobby or Jimmy, the main topic of conversation always ending up being Jesus. Maybe one of them will ask her to the Homecoming Dance. Kathi and Patti have dates, but Nanci doesn't yet. If Nanci doesn't get asked, Jill will go to the dance with her, and *vice versa*, though neither would go alone. The best-case scenario, an event as likely as an outbreak of world peace, is that Bobby Sawyer (Nanci's secret heartthrob) will ask her, and Rusty Boykin will ask Jill, but they're not even in the same group at all, except in academics.

Rusty gets into trouble a lot at school, but Jill has seen another side of him. Take that time he yelled at Chuckie Cooper when Chuckie was making fun of Camilla Creel.

Poor Camilla. Seems like every culture must have its scapegoats, and since elementary school, Camilla has been the punching-bag pariah of Green Wave country. Almost everyone refers to her as Fang behind her back. Last year, on St. Patrick's Day in the hall, Chuckie Cooper with that snarling grin of his actually said, "Top of the morning to you, Fang," as Camilla walked by, and, of course, there was a hail of laughter, and once Camilla was out of earshot, Rusty turned to Chuckie and said, "Wow, man, that was really courageous. Why don't you drive to the Habilitation Center this afternoon after practice? They have some micro-cephalics up there you can make fun of." Of course, Chuckie, who's real popular, was taken aback and said something vulgar suggesting Rusty has "done it" with Camilla, and Rusty responded by pulling on his left earlobe and saying "Right-O" in a fake English accent, and everybody laughed, because it was so unexpected, and it was, like, Rusty had won, because everyone knows that Rusty has never "done it" with Camilla. What Chuckie had said was, if not cowardly, mean. Chuckie lost his temper and came at Rusty, and Rusty said, "Please hit me, Chuckie, so AJ's daddy and me can divvy up your family's assets in a lawsuit, so I can get these teeth of mine fixed and you pay for them." Then Rusty smiled sarcastically the smile you give the dentist, and it stopped Chuckie right in his tracks. Chuckie pushed Rusty against the lockers and swore he wouldn't forget, and then Rusty turned to Jill and said, "Miss Birdsong, if something unfortunate happens to me in the near future, say, I disappear, please note this encounter when the police come around here asking questions." And that's when Jill's crush for Rusty really started, but she knows that there's no way he's going to ask her out, and if one of the Young Life guys asks her to the dance, she might just say no, because she wouldn't want to go and leave Nanci alone without a date.

***

Rusty's headed back to the art room. He almost forgot that he has an English essay due next period, and it's somewhere stashed among the papers in his bookbag he's left back there, along with his denim jacket. He wants to give the essay ("Too Small for His Britches: the Garment Motif in *Macbeth*") to somebody to turn in for him so Mrs. Barrineau won't smack him with a 10-point late penalty. As he scurries across the quad, he sees Mrs. Campbell, his favorite teacher from last year, with her arm around Dana Richards, all hunched over in a posture of complete demoralization. It probably has something to do with poor old Tripp. You know, things could be worse, like Will always says. He, Rusty, could be Tripp—or in Tripp's present state, no longer Tripp—and the absurdity of the thought, his feeling lucky to be a person he's not who isn't even a person anymore, makes Rusty sort of grimly chuckle. Unlike AJ, though, he's not going to openly mock the dead. When AJ had first heard the news, he immediately started making fun of Tripp. "What do you expect," AJ said, "if your last name is Trotter and you name your kid Tripp? He falls to his death. Surprise, surprise." AJ's flippancy shocked Will and some of the others. Sure, Tripp could be a jerk; he was a maniac, in fact. A jealous fiend. At Tastee Freeze Rusty had seen Tripp threaten Tommy Tuttle for

82

allegedly looking at Sandy. Still, Tripp's death is a tragedy. Well, if not exactly a tragedy in the literary sense, at least sad, not something you should mock.

When he arrives at the art room, Rusty sneaks a quick glance at himself in the reflection in the tinted glass of the narrow pane of the door, an image he approves of because it lacks pimples but reflects the halo of his doomed-to-be-shorn red hair, hair that refuses to stay combed. He enters the studio, gathers his books, and puts on his blue jean jacket. "Um, Mizz Turlock," he says. "I've been kicked out of school until I get a haircut and change my clothes, and I was wondering if I could ask you for some advice, if you don't mind."

"Of course, Rusty, if I can."

"I got this essay due to Mrs. Barrineau next period, and I was wondering if you thought Mrs. Barrineau would get mad at me if I interrupted her class to deliver it to her, because, if I don't, it'll be late."

Becky has no earthly idea. "I'll tell you what, Rusty. Give it to me, and I'll make sure she gets it. I'll explain the situation."

"Oh man, thanks," he says. "I'm in enough trouble as it is."

As Rusty beats his hasty exit, the class needs to be told to settle down. Althea turns to James. "The poor boy doesn't have a car. He rides to school with AJ."

"I wonder if his mom will be mad."

"Like, wouldn't she have to be aware that he's out of dress code?"

"You'd think."

"Hey, James, would you look at this a sec?"

Theatrically, gracefully, he leans over to look at Althea's sketch, a series of ovals, the large one, he supposes the ring of the coliseum/stadium, a swatch of thickly populated ovals to the left representing the spectators in the stands, and then the inner ovals: the gladiators, lions, whatever.

"I'm worried about perspective, the proportions," Althea says. The loose dress she's wearing is an off-white muslin thingy, layered with a matching scarf that is draped around her neck, Jagger-style, though James can't think of two more dissimilar physiques, and frankly, there is too much there, both in the costuming and the wearer.

"You, know," James says, "getting perspective correct in this piece isn't worth it. You'd have to do the math, grid it. If it's a little bit distorted, that's sort of the point, isn't it? These people are warped. They pull kids out of classes and put them out on the street to go get haircuts. And they're the adults! I'd do it like a political cartoon. Oh, don't frown. No, I mean like what's-his-name, that English painter, starts with an H, Holbrook, something like that. Wait one sec."

He gets up and glides over to Miss Turlock's desk. She's reading something, a paper, and doesn't see him at first. He sort of clears his voice; she looks up, embarrassed. "Excuse me, Miss Turlock, but I'm trying to remember a painter's name. He was English. Starts with an H. Did those caricature-like paintings, paintings of insane asylums and such."

"Hogarth?"

"That's it," James says, making little quiet clapping gestures. "Allie's worried about perspective, and I suggested she do her painting in, how do you say it, in a Hogarthian style."

"Great idea James! Let's see…". She's rising from behind the desk where James glances down and sees Rusty's essay open with its yucky, ink-smeared, inelegant handwriting. "I'm pretty sure Hogarth is in one of my books. Run over and fetch Althea, and I'll see if I can find it."

There's a narrow seven-foot metal bookcase behind her cattycornered desk where she keeps three or four art history tomes and other assorted college texts she'd rather store here at school. Flipping through the index of the first one she opens, she looks up, smiles, and says out loud, "Eureka!" She waves her hand, excitedly beckoning James and Althea to come over and have a look. Althea might just be able to pull this off, and Becky could make sure that it makes the cut in the annual spring art show where it would be prominently displayed. She flips through the pages pointing out the paintings, some of them devoted to rather odd subjects.

"I think a Hogarthian style would be perfect for a satiric painting," Becky says, "because I remember an old art professor of mine calling Hogarth 'the Jonathan Swift of painting.'"

"You know Swift, don't you?"

"Sort of," James says. "He's the one that wrote *Gulliver's Travels*, right?"

"Yeah, but that's tame stuff compared to some of the things he wrote."

"Anyway, look at these two paintings." She points to a color plate depicting an 18th century couple in wigs and rumpled period costumes sprawled on a bench in a park. "This one's called *After*. What's going on here?"

"I don't know; have they been robbed?" Althea asks.

"Looks like they've just done it," James says giggling.

"Exactly," Miss Trulock says, nodding enthusiastically. Now look at this one. She points to another plate called *The Denunciation*, an out-of-perspective depiction of a courtroom where a frowning pregnant woman in profile is being denounced by a fat judge in a silly white wig.

James and Althea go "Wow!" simultaneously and look at each other laughing.

Althea seems pleased, and the two retreat to their table as Becky returns to her seat and continues to read:

Too Small for his Britches:
the Garment Motif in *Macbeth*

Unlike *Hamlet*, that play that goes nowhere "slow," *Macbeth* enjoys a short, well-constructed plot that could conceivably be a "two-hours" traffic of the "stage," yet, nevertheless, the so-called Bard of Avon has supplied the play with a generous shipment of garment images to tie the entire drama together as a unifying device. Indeed, when one reads the play, one can see that images of garments demonstrate, or rather, reinforces, what's going on in the drama, whether it be early when Macbeth has broken in his Levis, as it were, or in the middle when he's more comfortable in them, but especially near the end when it is obvious that, ironically, he has been found to be "too small for his britches," that is unable to fill the royal shoes of the slain Duncan […]

Becky discreetly closes the essay, folded lengthwise. You couldn't pay her enough to be an English teacher.

***

Dana Richards, her tears finally under control, sits in Mrs. Palmer's office on a loveseat with a box of Kleenex in her lap, her handbag next to her. Josephine Palmer has been the guidance counselor at Summerville High ever since there's been a guidance counselor, the Martha Washington of guidance counselors, you might say, which she *has* said and *does* say. In her years of counseling, which usually amounts to administering personality and vocational suitability tests or providing college applications for state-supported colleges and universities, Mrs. Palmer hasn't had many crises: two unwed mothers, the death of a few parents, the death of one sibling. She's not been exactly trained as a grief counselor. However, she is a woman of abundant commonsense, and her intuition tells her that something more than grief is going on here.

She has pulled a chair opposite to Dana on the loveseat. "Now, honey," she says, sitting down. "Is something troubling you besides Tripp's accident? It's been a while now, and most people, after a week's time, don't react so strongly to the loss of a friend, you know?"

Dana's eyes are puffy, her mascara and eyeliner smeared, her nostrils glistening. "It just scares me so," she manages, looking down.

"Well," Mrs. Palmer acknowledges, "of course, death is frightening, but in Tripp's case, well, his death, it was avoidable. He really made a very bad decision. I know that you're a smart and careful girl. I've seen your achievement test scores, and I'm confident that you'd never do a foolish thing like fall off a bridge in the middle of the night."

"No, Ma'am. I wouldn't."

"Well then, honey, if you avoid making bad decisions, if you don't smoke cigarettes, avoid alcoholic beverages, and drive safely, there's no reason to think that you won't live a long and happy life—the seventy-two-year life expectancy of an average American female at least."

Dana looks up and sees that Mrs. Palmer's smiling confidently.

"That's not why I'm scared. I'm not afraid that *I'm* going to die."

"Then what are you afraid of?"

"I'm not supposed to say. I promised not to say."

"Promised who?"

"I mean I promised me."

Mrs. Palmer has leaned over and with her right hand has gently lifted Dana's chin so that their eyes meet. Again, Dana's are swelling with tears. "Look," Mrs. Palmer says, "if you're worried about Sandy, you better tell me, Dana. You're a child, and I am an adult, trained to deal with situations like this. You have to tell me. If anything bad happened to Sandy and you could have prevented it by telling me, you'd never be able to forgive yourself. Now tell me, Dana, what are you scared of."

And now it's pouring out of her. She retrieves the note, its well-thumbed stationary soft. Mrs. Palmer reaches for the reading glasses that dangle like a necklace at the swell of her bust. She scans the note hurriedly once and now reads it again slowly.

"When's the last time you talked to Sandy?" she asks, fingering the chain of her reading glasses.

"Last night?"

"Late last night?" Dana has surrendered. It's too much for her. She wants to go back home crawl under the covers, move to Argentina, to disappear.

"About ten."

"When did you get this note?"

"This morning."

"Sandy didn't give it to you?"

"No, one of Sandy's friends. A boy I don't know. He's from Charleston. He's in the band we're trying to get for the dance."

"Stay right here, honey," Jo Palmer says, "I'm so, so proud of you. You don't know how proud of you I am. I'll be right back."

***

On the north side of South Carolina Highway 17-A just around a curve from a two-story high school, a redheaded sixteen-year-old boy in a silk-screened blue jean jacket walks backward with his thumb thrust out. Inside the school, another sixteen-year-old boy, this one dark-haired and wearing wirerimmed glasses, translates a passage from *Don Quixote*. A mile and a half to the east as the crow flies, a basset hound with a red collar zigzags his way toward Bacons Bridge Road, a route that merges with Highway 61, crosses the Ashley River, then runs parallel to the river through a scenic tunnel of moss-draped oaks where antebellum plantations and gardens attract tourists in the spring. Meanwhile in one of the growing housing developments just outside the quaint town of Summerville, a middle-aged woman in a pink robe fills a tomato-stained glass with tap water and leaves it in the sink. Back at the school, a younger, plumper woman chastises a hyper Jewish kid with braces. Another set of ancient oaks embower a driveway where a maroon VW bus and a white VW bug follow one another out onto Carolina Avenue in the verdant heart of Old Summerville. Back at the school, two students are putting their art supplies away in anticipation of the end of class while a red Mustang hurtles in the opposite direction of—and past—the redheaded hitchhiker. The Mustang slams on brakes, does a screeching, tire-smoking 180, and slides to a stop in the opposite lane. Startled, the redheaded boy does a nervous little Chaplinesque dance as electricity whiplashes in a rush up his spine. He suddenly realizes that it's *her* car, hears *her* New Jersey accent calling his name, asking him where he's headed, inviting him to hop on in, and he begins to run toward the passenger side door. Around the curve at the school, a series of electric bells go

RRRRRRRIIIIIIIIIIIIIIIIIINNNNNNNNNNNG!!!

and a tall, slender math student picks up her things to head to English while on the first floor directly under her classroom, an orange-haired typist clumsily removes a sheet of onion paper from a typewriter that has seen better days.

Third Period

Third Period (9:50–10:35 A.M.)

Many consider Frances Barrineau the finest teacher at Summerville High. She's demanding but fair and produces literate graduates who write tightly unified five-paragraph essays. An alumna of Wellesley, she married a UVA grad, now the general manager of the Charleston, South Carolina division of West Virginia Pulp and Paper Company, the second largest employer in the Tri-County Area. A predominant polluter, WVP&P spews noxious industrial flatulence whose odors, under certain atmospheric conditions, can be detected as far away as Summerville, a good fifteen miles northwest of its spewing smokestacks. "Smells like bread and butter to me," Frances says with a twinkle in her eye.

The class that sits before her is her second favorite, English IV, British Literature, a mixture of advanced juniors and regular seniors. Not surprisingly, Frances Barrineau's Advanced Seminar for seniors ranks as her favorite class, but the juniors sitting here constitute a particularly good crop. As instructed, each student has opened his or her textbook to page 241, Act 5, Scene 3 of *Macbeth*. All but Rusty Boykin, that is. Becky Turlock has just delivered his essay, which looks as if it may have weathered a journey from Samarqand on camel back. Folded lengthwise (as instructed), the paper is wrinkled, the edges curling; however, Rusty's juvenile handwriting with class information *is* scrawled on the right facing side (as instructed). Sighing, her fountain pen in hand, Mrs. Barrineau makes a note on a personalized pad (both pen and pad gifts from graduating seniors). She's reminded herself to offer a witticism about Pope's *Rape of the Lock* when Rusty returns. She regrets, though, his absence because he has enthusiastically reacted to the play. Students who love literature are a rare species, the painted buntings of adolescent academia, but Rusty's always too much in a hurry and terribly immature.

Jill Birdsong and a delighted Jackie Geat are also aware that Rusty's assigned seat is empty. Ollie Wyborn, who overheard hall gossip regarding Rusty's absence, is perplexed at both the administration's and Rusty's pettiness over something as unimportant as the length of one's hair. After all, hair is just keratin, long polymers of amino acids protruding through the epidermis of the scalp. (Scientists disagree about its function; Fisherian runaway sexual selection is Ollie's best guess). Ollie senses his heart rate is slightly elevated as he glances across two rows of desks at Jill Birdsong, sitting in profile, writing something in the composition book next to her open text.

Actually, she's doodling, her mind wandering as she sketches little bunny rabbits with long bunny rabbit ears. Mrs. Barrineau, eager to begin, steps out from behind her podium. Sporting a brown and gold checkered woolen skirt, a pale-yellow silk blouse, and a cameo pinned at her neck, she's a handsome woman in her mid-fifties with expensively coiffed, strikingly white hair. Her smile is a bit crooked, which sometimes seems playful, other times sardonic. She touches the side frame of her bifocals—a nervous habit—before she starts to take up the essays, one by one, asking each student which motif he or she chose.

Once the essays have been safely bound by a red rubber band, she asks Jackie Geat to read Macbeth's "[…] my way of life/Has fallen into the sear/The yellow leaf" speech. Jackie moves her head from side to side and gives a bravura performance with a slight British *Masterpiece Theater* inflection that prompts Rozier Ravenel to glance over to Steve Murray, who's turning red and stifling a giggle.

"Class, what adjectives come to mind when trying to describe the tone of the speech?"

Cindy Cauthen: "Despairing."

Ollie Wyborn: "Woebegone."

"How about you, Jill?"

"Resigned."

***

Inez Johnson, Police Chief John Bigelow's secretary, puts down her lipstick-red-ringed Winston to answer the telephone. John's sitting across the office with his motorcycle boots propped on his paper-strewn desk, and he's smoking an unfiltered Camel while he reads the local section of the *News and Courier*. A haze of cigarette smoke perpetually hovers in police headquarters. In fact, a film of yellow nicotine coats the windows. Crackling in the corner, a four-way radio periodically blares Officer Dickey's and

Officer Applegate's "ten-fours" and "rogers" as they patrol the generally quiet streets, or just as frequently, lounge at Eva's Sweet Shop or the poolhall, which can occasionally be the scene of a broken nose, bloody lip, or black eye, especially now that some of the kids are growing their hair and dressing like hobos. Knightsville and Stallsville boys aren't big fans of freedom of expression.

"John, it's Paul Pushcart," Inez says, "line one."

A heavy sigh. "Bigelow here. Uh-huh," he says in his hoarse, gravelly voice. His coloring is just this side of gray, and large dark bags bulge beneath his unhappy brown eyes. He looks as if he hasn't had a good night's sleep since World War II.

Inez is on her third Coca-Cola and tenth cigarette of the day. Her nails, sculpted and red, match her lipstick. She herself sighs. John's habit of saying "Uh-huh" over and over and over again can get to be really, really, really irritating.

"Uh-huh."

He's the most hush-mouth man she's ever been around. Makes her ex-husband Bubba look like a chatterbox in comparison. No wonder John's wife Maureen never smiles.

"Uh-huh."

Inez and Bigelow can sit in that office sometimes an hour at a time, and he never says a word. Of all the words he's ever uttered, "uh-huh" must outnumber the rest fifteen to one.

"Uh-huh."

One day, bored to death, she marked on a notepad each time he said "uh-huh" – four vertical slashes and then a fifth struck through on top designating a bundle of five. Seventy-seven "uh-huhs" in one conversation.

"Uh-huh. Okay, I'll see what I can do." He slams down the phone.

"What's the matter now?" Inez asks.

"Damn teenagers."

He lumbers over to the radio, snatches up the mike and presses the red button on its side.

"Dickey, Bigelow. I want you to be on the lookout for a red '69 Mustang, South Carolina license tag number KLP 856, driven by a white female, age sixteen."

"That's a ten-four."

"If you see her, pull her over and contact me."

"What's that tag number again?"

"KLP 856." K – as in Kentucky, L – as in Louisiana, P – as in Pennsylvania. Eight. Five. Six.

"Roger. What's she done?"

"Over and out."

***

Once Sandy's red Mustang has skidded to a stop, she shouts, "Hey, Rusty, whatcha doing? Escaping from Alcatraz?" Sandy's so popular that some of the girls have started affecting New Jersey accents. "Whatcha think of my patented bat turn?"

"Wow," is all he can manage.

"Well, just don't stand there. Hop in."

"Thanks," he says, opening the door, settling in. "I wouldn't say I'm escaping, but it's more like I'm in exile. Booted out for numerous and sundry dress code violations."

She squeals off, headed back toward town, lurching Rusty back into the white leather bucket seat. Even though it's still in the mid-sixties outside, Sandy has the windows rolled down, so their hair whips in the wind. He feels awkward, thinks he should offer her condolences, but everything he thinks of sounds so lame:

"Sorry about Tripp."

"Tough break about Tripp."

"Alas, poor Tripp!"

As he's about to take a stab, she suddenly asks, "Hey, Rusty, you think there's a God?"

It's a question that has plagued Rusty since kindergarten. He's always wanted to believe in God, especially in Jesus, and envies those who do, because having a celestial parent who provides cosmic justice that results in eternal life makes human suffering tolerable. After confirmation classes four years ago, it was almost as if he really believed – at least for a week or two – but the conviction didn't last.

Rusty figures that the last thing someone wants to hear after her boyfriend has died is that God is a myth, that there's no such thing as an afterlife. On the other hand, considering Tripp's assholedom, mere oblivion with no hellish consequences might not be such a bad thing. "I hate to say this," Rusty answers, shouting over the wind roar, "because of Tripp and all, but I have never believed in God, not really. Man, Sandy, I'm really sorry about what happened. I've been thinking about you a lot. Everyone has."

Sandy stares straight ahead, her hair streaming back. "So, you don't believe in God?"

"Not even when I was little, I didn't," he admits, leaning closer to her in the wind, further raising his voice.

"It's funny since I believed in Santa Claus and flying reindeer. Elves. The North Pole. Circumnavigating the globe. I believed in all that, but I didn't believe in the Old Testament God.

"I remember when I was around five being in Miss Marion's kindergarten. She began each day with a Bible story. We'd sit in a little semicircle on the floor, and she stood in front of this gigantic picture book propped up on an easel. She'd turn the pages while she read, going slowly, giving us time to check out the illustrations so we could see the animals two by two, marching into in the ark, aardvarks, zebras, dormice. I remember thinking to my tiny little innocent self, 'Hey, man, that's bullshit.' Well, of course, I didn't think *bullshit*, or *man*, or even *puppy poop* for that matter; maybe I thought *malarkey*. But, anyway, I just instinctively knew that it couldn't be true."

While he's talking, Rusty's facing Sandy's profile, watching strands of her loosened hair snaking out in the breeze. Embarrassed, he glances out of his window at the green blur rushing past. When he turns back, she's smiling.

"I don't believe in God either. You didn't go to Tripp's funeral, did you?" She doesn't ask it accusingly or bitterly or disappointedly or even sadly.

"No," Rusty admits. "I missed it," and again he looks away.

"Well, at the funeral Pastor Hale kept saying that Tripp was in heaven hunting and fishing and that we'd all meet again one day, but I hate hunting and fishing. It's so cruel, shooting those beautiful deer, and the thing is, Tripp's not hunting or fishing. He's dead. Laying in that coffin."

He has turned again to face her, expecting tears, but she seems composed. "I hasten to add," Rusty says, playing it safe, "that just because I don't believe doesn't make it *not* so. Maybe those old Bible stories were created for primitives, sheepherders, illiterate nomads, because fairy tales were all they could understand. If there's a God, though, it's not going to be a He but a Force or something. So, I agree with you. There's no way Tripp's plugging some deer with some heavenly firearm or Humphrey Bogart's downing scotch in some heavenly night club or my dead grandmama's shelling snap beans on some heavenly front porch with Aunt Polly."

"So, you don't hunt or fish?"

"No, I'm a real pu—uh, a real sissy when it comes to things like guns and chainsaws. They terrify me."

Sandy laughs out loud.

"Hey, Sandy," Rusty says. "Can I ask a favor? Would mind taking me to Will Waring's, so I can pick up something before I get a haircut?"

"Oh, don't cut that hair," she says, reaching over and patting his head, her hand pressing down and releasing, the hair flattening but then springing back, which causes the beatnik in his brain to start banging bongos. An oldie, "Tracks of My Tears," comes on the radio, but Rusty can hardly hear it because of the roar of the wind. He leans over and without asking jacks up the volume. "I really dig this song," he says, "the great Smoky Robinson."

The dashboard clock reads ten o'clock.

Will looks back in his rearview mirror to make sure that AJ's Bug is still behind him. Whenever he's stoned, AJ drives like those ancient men and women of Summerville who took their driving tests in Model T's, who peer beneath their steering wheels, who drive twenty miles-per-hour in a fifty-five zone. AJ also has a terrible sense of direction. Even though AJ's been to Eddie's summer place twice, he'd never be able to find it by himself unless he followed Will. Sometimes Will feels like a babysitter when he's dealing with AJ.

Eddie's country house is located two miles north of Bacons Bridge on the Ashley River. It's a two-story brick house built in the 1840s, only about 2,000 square feet, closet-less with twelve-foot ceilings, plaster walls, and warped pine floors. There's no insulation or central heat or air, just window fans and fireplaces. The Jenrettes and Warings have come here for generations to hunt and fish and water-ski, and, depending on how old they are, to get drunk or lose their virginity or have extramarital affairs or eventually (as in the case of Paw-Paw) to drop dead from a massive coronary. There's a boat ramp plus an old green rusted-out Ford truck suitable for hauling. If the place were in Charleston County, the Preservation Society would demand the Jenrettes restore the house, but Dorchester County's motto is the less government, the better. Absurdly enough, *Minor Ordinato, Major Bonum* appears on the seals of the county police cruisers underneath a crude likeness of Fort Dorchester, an 18th Century fortress constructed of oyster shells, now a ruin.

Again, Will checks his rearview and discovers to his consternation that AJ has pulled off on the side of the road. "What the?" The visibility out of his bus is horrible, and there's no easy way to turn around with water-filled ditches lining both sides of the highway. Another glance reveals that AJ's out of the car running around on the shoulder of the pavement. Will continues slowly ahead until he sees a couple of reflectors stuck into the ground on either side an unpaved driveway. He pulls in, opens his driver side door to look out up the highway, turns the balky steering wheel to the right and backs up to head back toward AJ.

By the time he's making forward progress, he sees AJ's VW back on the road heading toward Eddie's place. "Whoa!" Will yells, mashing on the horn that hasn't worked since he bought the bus. AJ, oblivious, passes right by him with—what's that? —with a dog sitting in the passenger seat. AJ's not watching where he's going, not noticing that Will has passed in the opposite direction but has his head turned to the dog, his mouth moving. He's talking to the dog like the dog can understand him, like he's Mr. Peabody from the Bullwinkle cartoons or Lassie or Rin Tin Tin.

Will slows down, looking for another spot where he can turn around. He has an 8-track tape player in the bus blaring Hendrix's "All Along the Watchtower." The good news is that AJ's going 35 in a 55-mph zone. Catching up and passing him will not be a problem.

"Businessmen," Will sings, "drink my wine. /Plowmen dig my herb."

***

Mr. Carpenter, the shop teacher – his name the source of many a joke – is a short, kindly man in his late forties. He prides himself in preparing his students for the real world, giving them a shot at getting a job at the Navy Yard, a secure place for life with government healthcare and a pension. Or they can get jobs in construction. The Tri-County Area is growing by leaps and bounds.

Some of these boys are hard cases, the ones from out in the country, especially. Like that Bosheen boy. His daddy is no damn good, in and out of jail, known to beat his wife. Mr. Carpenter recalls the conversation he recently overheard Bobbey Ray having with Bucky Gaskins. Something about giving somebody a haircut. Something about the poolhall. Something about after practice. Later, he called Bobbey Ray over and told him, "Look, bubba, I don't want to hear about anyone in this school getting a haircut that they didn't pay for. We've had enough trauma round here lately. We need you on that football field Friday. What you talking about could get you expelled or land you in jail."

"Mr. Carpenter," Bobbey Ray said, "I just cutting fool. I ain't giving nobody no haircut. They be a few what could use one, though."

***

Unlike many English teachers, Frances Barrineau doesn't have students reconstruct plays by assigning each student a role to read. If she has a student read a passage, it is to analyze the passage's meaning or poetic techniques. She sometimes requires students to scan the metrics to see if the iambic pentameter is regular. She expects her charges to have read their assignments, and almost always, most of them have. She has reached her absolute favorite lines of the play, and because of the recent tragic events, the lines should really reverberate with these bright young people. The speech is seared into her consciousness, and she won't allow the children to botch the lines. She'll recite them herself, walking into the students' space, into the center of the middle aisle, glancing at each boy and girl to assess reactions.

Out, out brief candle,
Life is but a walking shadow,
A poor player that struts and frets
His hour upon the stage and is heard no more.
It is a tale told by an idiot
Full of sound and fury
Signifying nothing.

The class is utterly silent.
"James," Mrs. Barrineau finally asks, "out, out what?"
"Brief candle."
"Brief candle. James, tell me what you see when I say, 'brief candle?' What image forms in your mind's eye?"
Despite being a target for bullies, James is not shy. He thinks for a second. "I see a medieval taper flickering in a castle." He makes a clicking noise with his tongue, a nervous habit that does not endear him to others.
"It could go out any second, right?"
"Yes, Ma'am and does," he says, thinking smugly of un-dear departed Tripp who was not kind to James Hopper

throughout their time together in the Summerville school system. Tripp's harassment of James coarsened throughout the years starting with "girl" in first grade, sharpening to "sissy" in third, morphing to "fairy" in sixth, hitting "queer" in Junior High, and culminating with "fucking faggot" just two weeks ago.

"It certainly does," Mrs. Barrineau says with a sad shake of her head. "We can all attest to that, given the tragic events of last week. And yet there is a paradox at play here. The days, each like the other, drag on, and yet life seems short. Despite the 'tomorrow, tomorrow, tomorrow,' the sameness of it all—what Walker Percy calls 'everydayness'—we turn around and—poof—it's over. Our lives are over! How can we explain this paradox?"

Mrs. Barrineau means it to be an unanswerable question, but now she sees that Ollie Wyborn has his hand up. "Yes, Ollie?"

"I think I can explain the paradox."

"Yes? You can?"

"It's because as we get older, our frame of reference for measuring time becomes smaller. For example, when I was three years old, my frame of reference was a year; it was a third of my life. An eternity, so to speak. If I'm eighty years old, a year is one eightieth of my life. A snap of the fingers. You know, when I was rereading this passage last night, I thought Shakespeare had erred. 'Brief candle' and 'tomorrow, tomorrow, and tomorrow' seemed contradictory, not a mixed metaphor, but something that doesn't fit. But now it does make sense. It's the sameness that makes it seem quick, the same routines, day after day after day, blending all together in an indistinguishable blur."

"Yes, Ollie, you may very well be right about that. Jackie?"

"Mrs. Barrineau, when I was working on my essay last night, my mother told me that Shakespeare really didn't write these plays."

"That's an old canard, Jackie. Trust me, he wrote them."

"She says that it wouldn't be possible for a peasant who couldn't spell his own last name to write these masterpieces full of technical information about the king and queen and legal matters and all that stuff."

"They're also full of homey everyday matters that aristocrats wouldn't know about, like raising livestock, and, by the way, he was middle class, his father was a mayor, he received a coat of arms in his later life. We don't have time to get into this now, but trust me, William Shakespeare wrote these plays!

"Now, the phrase, 'poor player.' What does he mean by that? Rozier, a poor quarterback? A poor shortstop?"

Rozier chuckles. "No, Ma'am. The footnote says he means an actor."

"Struts and frets. What's that? No one knows? What auditory device, I mean. No hands? I can't believe that no one can tell me this auditory term! Okay, Jill."

"Isn't it consonance?"

"Yes, consonance. Those are the words that stand out. 'Struts' like a bantam rooster; 'frets' like a worrywart. Then poof! It's over."

***

AJ's mother Anne, a tall thin fifty-year-old with salt-and-pepper hair, leads a life of leisure. Even though AJ is their only child (there were two miscarriages), the last thing you would call her and her husband is overprotective. In fact, she and Thom have been rather liberal in their child rearing, having read and applied Dr. Spock's permissive techniques. When Miss Cartwright called a few moments ago to ask Anne if AJ was at her house, her first reaction wasn't oh-my-god-something's-happened but more like here-we-go-again. She listened patiently and then hung up after promising to contact the school as soon as she heard from him. She considered calling Thom at the office but was fairly certain he had court today and wouldn't be in. She returned to the sitting room where she had been reading the paper and listening to Chopin's Ballade No. 3 in A flat Major. She sat thinking, looking out of the window at the magnolia and its shade, all of those irritating leaves that forever seem to be shedding. Thom had wanted to ship AJ off to Woodberry Forest, his alma mater, but she wouldn't part with her only child so soon. Maybe she was wrong about sending him to SHS. Despite his 145 IQ, AJ's grades have been mediocre. He isn't even in the honors classes and is getting into more and more trouble. But really, it is all innocent trouble, impertinence and intemperance. Sitting there, she weighed her options about what to do, if anything. Glancing at her watch, she sees it's after ten. Maybe she should call the poolhall or Will's mom. Or why not just cut right to the chase and call Will himself? If he wasn't up by now, it was high time he was. If he were her son and had dropped out of school, she'd have him working forty hours a week and paying rent. Or would she? Probably not. She'd probably send him off to boarding school, even if it were for only one year.

***

Tooling north on Main Street in his black and white cruiser, Officer Mickey Dickey relishes the idea of tracking down some spoiled brat teenage bitch in a bright red Mustang. He recalls a movie he saw a while ago featuring drug-crazed sex maniacs with short skirts, cavorting in convertibles with psychedelic music screeching from their radios. Seems like after that boy lost his life, they might learn a lesson. Dickey bets LSD did Tripp in. Like Art Linkletter's daughter, the fool probably thought he was a bird or something, took off flapping his arms, and plopped right down on that stump, shattering his skull.

Dickey considers sparing the rod as the source of the problem with today's young'uns. Dickey himself prefers the belt. When they were little, if one of his own gave him any lip—smack—and that was that. They'd turned out all right, Brandon in his second tour of duty in Nam and Brandi married with a daughter of her own.

Dickey decides to pull up at the poolhall to see if Buzz has any information, because that goddamn John Bigelow sure as hell won't share any. *Over and out.* Son-of-a-bitch. Dickey is six-foot-even, fat and with a head that's wider at the jaw than at the eyeline. His belly and the steering wheel have formed an uneasy alliance. As he pulls to a stop, yanks out the keys, and reaches for the door handle, he's already panting, emerging from the cruiser laden with the tools of his trade: handcuffs, billy club, pistol, bullet belt, badge.

Across the street, two-hundred-year-old oaks grace Summerville's town square, a green space with azaleas and park benches located between North and South Main. On the poolhall side of the square, parking is parallel, not diagonal like on the other side, in front old the more prestigious stores: Guerrins Pharmacy, Dorchester Jewelers, Barshay's, and Alexander's Department Store.

T & T Sporting Center, commonly known as the poolhall, is owned by Peter and Margaret Marconi, both in their sixties, and operated by their son, Buzz, who though only thirty seems older with his salt-and-pepper hair. He always wears black, a black pullover and black chinos or jeans. He's a graduate of Appalachian State, a university in the mountains of western North Carolina, which he attended via the GI Bill after serving four years in the Navy. Buzz has seen the wide, wide world and countless curiosities, from radiation-damaged mutants in Nagasaki to gun-toting commies down in Panama. He cultivates a Hemingway-like mystique. It's as if coming back to settle down in Summerville is a diminishment, but he's married with three kids already, all boys. The young people who hang at the poolhall respect Buzz, as much for his biceps and upper body strength as for his exotic travelogues. Some, like Rusty, seek his advice on occasion.

"Whatcha say?" Buzz says as Dickey waddles up to one of the red bar stools.

"Hey, Buzz. How about a couple of hotdogs?"

"Starting pretty early," Buzz says with a grin.

The poolhall is practically empty, except for Eddie Jenrette and Hank Pritchard engaged in a friendly game of 6-ball on Table 1.

Buzz retrieves the hotdogs, places them in buns and then paper sleeves, ladling the secret special chili over the franks. Although not asked to, Buzz opens a bottle of Coke. Rooting in his pocket, Dickey pulls out a one and slaps it on the bar.

"It's a dollar and three cents," Buzz says. "The three cents pays your salary."

"That three cents goes to the school, bubba."

"Details, details."

"Hey, Buzz," Dickey says, fishing the pennies out of his pockets. "You know any little high school honey that drives a red Mustang?"

"I don't see what they drive up in. Besides, when have you ever seen a girl in here?"

"Just checking. You reckon either of them fellows knows?"

"Hey, Eddie," Buzz shouts, "You know any babe who drives a red Mustang?"

Eddie, who's chalking his cue, looks over and sees Dickey sitting at the counter. "Can't help you there. Hank, you know of any?" Leaning over the table, Hank looks up from his shot, shaking his head.

"Itn't that that Jenrette boy?" Dickey asks, chomping down on his dog, leaning over the counter and dribbling chili.

"Yeah, he's 'taking a semester off' from Carolina."

"That so."

"Staying out at the old plantation till it gets too cold."

"That so. Officer Harrison might be interested to know that." Officer Harrison is the town's newly hired narcotics officer.

"You best not mess with the Jenrettes, bo."

"Oh yeah?"

"Ask the Mayor if you don't believe me."

"What's that supposed to mean?"

"Nothing. Just ask him."

"Look at that jackass," Eddie says, meaning Dickey, as Eddie signals to Buzz that he owes for another game but is going to rack the balls himself so save Buzz the trip.

Although Eddie Jenrette is Will Waring's first cousin, they look nothing alike. Eddie's dark, brown-eyed, and handsome, though his hair is already receding at twenty-two. He's wild with a dry wit but possesses a good deal of common sense. He's a realist, not a romantic, unlike Cousin Will and Rusty Boykin.

"Tripp's girlfriend drove a red Mustang, didn't she?" Hank asks.

"Drives," Eddie says, "she's not the dead one."

"I guess she's become available now, huh?"

"Listen to you," Eddie says, "going steady."

"I'm going steady," Hank says. "I ain't dead."

***

"Okay, Sandy, slow down," Rusty says as they approach the left-hand turn off to Will's. "See that brick wall. It's there. See it?" After she turns in, gravel crunches as the Mustang negotiates a slight incline, then levels out, slowly winding its way through overgrown camellias. With so much shade, grass is sparse. "Go on past the Big House," Rusty says. "See the carriage house over there. Park behind it, okay?"

Sandy pulls to a stop. "Oh, great," Rusty says, "his van's not here."

"What's it you need to pick up?"

"Actually, some money."

"What for? I got money." She leans over to her purse, roots through items looking for her wallet, then pulls out some prescription medication, rattling it like a maraca. "I also got these. They make you feel really good."

"What is it?"

"Something they gave me after Tripp died."

"They being doctors?"

"Yeah. Wanna try one?"

Sandy's leaning over toward Rusty, and she's looking earnestly, if not pleadingly, into his hazel eyes. The beatnik in his brain is, like, on bennies now, banging like a maniac on those bongos, trying to drown out his Inner Rationalist who contemplates mathematical averages and the righteous wrath of disappointed fathers.

"No thanks," he says. "Not right at this second. Come on in with me. I can probably scrape up enough for a haircut."

She follows him up the stairs, and he knocks on the door using the bottom of his fists instead of his knuckles.

"Like I said, I got money."

"I can't borrow money from you."

"Why not?"

He opens the door and shouts, "Will," but there is no answer, so he struggles to push the warped door open, scraping the wide planks of the blackened pine floor.

"Now I didn't catch why you can't borrow money from me?" Sandy says, glancing around the cluttered gloom of the room. The apartment smells funny, like perfume or something.

"I dunno. It's not chivalrous to borrow money from a girl, I guess."

"Is it chivalrous to borrow money from a boy?"

"Not really."

Rusty goes over to the turntable. "Hey, Sandy," he says, trying to change the subject. "Do you like the Beatles or the Stones better?"

"I like both okay," she says a bit hesitantly. "I don't buy records really. Hey, Rusty, you think Will would mind if I used his restroom?"

Rusty can't stand it when people call private bathrooms restrooms. He usually offers some sarcastic comment about taking naps on the cold piss-splattered floors beneath the urinals, but it doesn't even occur to him that Sandy has violated this peeve of his. "Sure, it's liable to be gross, though. It's through there around the corner. Make yourself at home."

As soon as she disappears, he rushes over to the sofa and removes its cushions, rummaging for change. In the bathroom, Sandy wonders if someone dropped and broke a bottle of cologne. The plumbing fixtures are ancient, the sink yellowed. She opens her purse, retrieves the pills and rattles out one. She turns on the tap, pops the pill, and leans over to the faucet to get a mouthful of water, making sure it's not rust-colored before she slurps. Turning off the spigot, she leans in look at herself in the old, grainy, smoky mirror. Now the spigot is dripping. As hard as she tries, she can't turn it tight enough to stop the plop plop plop. Music starts to play in the other room. She sits on the toilet, pulls up her skirt to see if maybe, just maybe there are signs. No luck. She gets up, takes another glance in the mirror.

When she finally comes out, Rusty's standing there, looking nervous with his hands in his pockets.

"You know what, Rusty? Why don't you let me give you a haircut? You know, with some gel I can make your hair look shorter than it is. I can show you how to fix it. You can groom it my way in the mornings, then, fluff it out after school. I can work miracles with hair."

"Wow, okay. But, man, we don't have any clippers or anything like that."

"All I need is scissors, and I have some in my glove compartment."

"You carry scissors in your glove compartment?"

"Yeah," she admits, "to trim split ends. I'm very vain about my hair. I know it's not a very admirable trait."

"Oh man," he says. "I don't blame you. It's gorgeous."

She smiles warmly. "I'll be right back."

The clock on the mantel now reads almost twenty after X. Rusty has thirty minutes to get this haircut, confiscate one of Will's shirts, and go roaring back to school so he can make a forty or a fifty on this midterm. His inner rationalist, now tapping his foot to the bongo beat, erases the board. A forty or fifty versus an afternoon with Sandy. He takes the Stones LP off the turntable, careful not to put his fingers on the grooves. Unlike Rusty, Will takes meticulous care of his records. Having been yelled at more than once, Rusty finds the jacket, slips the vinyl in, and then goes flipping through the stacks searching for Sgt. Pepper's. The door scrapes open, and there's Sandy, working the scissors with her left hand like a demented Harpo Marx, smiling, saying, "I can't wait to get my hands on those locks."

"How 'bout some music? You can cut hair to music, can't you?"

"I don't know," she says coyly. "Never tried it."

"Eureka, Sgt. Pepper's."

"Ever heard of this?" he asks, showing her the cover.

"I don't know. I think maybe."

"You've seen this cover, though, right?"

"I'm not sure."

He slides the vinyl disc out and puts on side 2, clicks the automatic play on the turntable and hands her the cover.

"This is very cool. Look, there's Tarzan," she says.

"And Edgar Alan Poe, and Laurel and Hardy."

"Maybe we ought to do it in the bathroom," Sandy says, handing the cover back to him, "so we don't get hair all over everything. By the way, what's with all these cats?"

"It's Will's mom. She doesn't have any of them fixed. I bet half of them are pregnant."

At this, Sandy frowns and Rusty wonders what he's said or done to upset her.

"What's the matter?"

And now, suddenly, she's crying, weeping big time, sobbing with scissors in her left hand, tears pouring down her face like they'd been dammed up and the levee has broken.

Instinctively, Rusty goes up to her and puts his arms around her, the way he might hug his scared little sister, and Sandy hugs him back, still holding the scissors, and now she's shaking with sobs, and Rusty's saying, "Crying's probably good for you," as if she hasn't been breaking down off and on like this for days.

All to the tune of "Within You, Without You."

The phone rings.

Instinctively, they part.

It rings again.

"You okay?"

Riiiiiiiiinnnnnnnnnnnnngggggggggggg.

"I guess so."

The bells, the bells, the bells, the bells.

"I'm gonna answer it," Rusty says. "It's driving me crazy."

"Okay,"

Riiiiiiiiinnnnnnnnnnnnngggggggggggg.

"Hello, Will Waring's residence."

Muffled talking on the other end.

"No, Ma'am. This is Rusty. Will's not here."

He's pantomiming to Sandy to show her the call's no big deal.

"No, Ma'am, I don't know where he is."

Sandy's tears have subsided, though she's still sniffling.

"Yes, Ma'am, I know. Uh-huh. I've sort of been kicked out of school myself. Uh-huh. No, just till I get my hair cut. Yes, Ma'am. That's what I'm fixing to do. Yes, Ma'am. Sure will. I'll let him know you're looking for him. You're welcome. I really don't think it's his fault. Okay. Yes, Ma'am. Goodbye."

"Who was that?"

"AJ's mama. He's disappeared."

"Disappeared."

"Joined the French Foreign Legion."

"Huh?"

"It's a joke."

Sandy's cheeks are flushed, and with that long hair she looks a little bit like an older woebegone Alice in Wonderland.

"Not that he's disappeared," Rusty says, "but that he's joined the Foreign Legion. Sorry, that wasn't a funny joke. His mama's not worried. She knows what a rapscallion he is. She's figured out that he's off with Will somewhere. Probably the poolhall."

"Rapscallion," Sandy repeats. "What a cool word. Are you a rapscallion?"

"Not really. I sort of wish I was. I'm just a crazy, mixed-up kid."

"Man, I can't follow half of what you say, but I like the way you say it."

"Thanks, Sandy! Some people find my highfalutin' lexicon off-putting. *C'est la vie* is what I say."

***

There's no avenue of oaks leading to up to the Jenrette plantation house, just a short, winding dirt road that opens to the brown brick edifice perched on the river's edge. Across the way, to the side, stand two detached wooden horse stables that have been converted to garages. The green truck is missing, but the boat trailer is parked in the garage with a twelve-foot aluminum jon boat perched upon it. Will's and AJ's Volkswagens, both produced in 1965, slowly wend their way toward the garages. AJ's burgundy bus has been souped up in grand style with a refitted interior that includes a bed and decoupaged walls displaying everything from Little Annie Fanny to mushroom clouds. AJ's white Bug, dented and decal plastered, follows. The vehicles pull to a stop; Will hops out while AJ and Hambone exit the Bug.

"What's the scoop on Mr. Peabody?" Will asks.

"Man, I nearly ran over this mutt. It darted out right in front of me. You didn't see it? Thank God I was only going seventeen miles per hour. I tell you this mutt owes me his life. Or her life."

"This is a basset hound, man. It's not a mutt. And let me show you how you can tell the sex of one of these animals. Look right here. You see those things down there? That's called a dick and some balls. If you see that on a dog, that means the dog's a male dog."

"Ha, ha, very funny."

Will leans over to look at the tag hanging from Mr. Peabody's red collar, just a rabies tag, no address. "Well, now we have ourselves an official mascot, Mr. Peabody. I'm gonna replace that collar with a bow tie. He can offer us sage advice on our adventures."

AJ, who is a crackerjack mimic, sounding just like Bullwinkle the Moose, says, "Hello there, tree people," and Will cracks up.

"Can you do the Mr. Peabody voice?" Will asks. "It's something like [nasally], 'Actually, Sherman, the square root of the hypotenuse.'"

"Actually, Sherman, the square root of the hypotenuse."

"Naw, that's not quite right. Mr. Peabody has a deep, adult voice. It's Sherman that talks through his nose."

"Anyway," AJ says, "back to the actual cartoon we're in. I guess we'll have to take him to a shelter or something."

"No, man. He can hang with us. I'll give him to Mama later, and she can put an ad in the paper. Maybe no one will claim him, and we can keep him. Might chase away a cat or two."

"He's a moaner, man. He was howling like a wounded water buffalo or something."

"Anyway, let's take a look at that boat trailer."

The temperature has risen a bit. Will has rolled up the sleeves of his green plaid flannel shirt.

"I dunno," AJ says. "You think the raft's gonna fit on that? I think it's too wide."

"The raft?"

"Yeah, it'll never fit on that."

"We'll make it work. Eddie'll help us. I was hoping against hope he'd be around here. I don't see his big truck or the green truck. Let's go see if he's in the house. Come on, Mr. Peabody, you can hang out in this bus." Will slides the side door open and coaxes Mr. Peabody into the bus. He slides the door shut.

"Hey, man. That's cruel."

"He'll run off and get run over if we leave him out here. The fate you saved him from. I suspect that this Mr. Peabody is looking for love."

A heartbreaking blues bellow issues from inside the bus, as if a monstrous birth is transpiring.

"Jesus Christ," Will says. "Hop in, AJ. We'll drive to the house." They pile into the bus, which Will coaxes to start after a backfire that has Alex jumping out of his skin.

"Oh, do Lawd," he says, mimicking Eva Mae, his childhood nursemaid.

Will pulls up next to the porch while AJ continues to fan himself like a swooning damsel.

The house is dark. No one responds to Will's knocking and shouting, so they get in the bus and drive back fifty yards to the garage through the dust they'd just kicked up.

"Well, now what?" AJ asks from the passenger seat.

"We'll take the boat off the trailer, hook the trailer to my bus, then go back to my pad to get the raft and bring it back here."

"You got a trailer hitch on the back of this thing?"

It hadn't occurred to Will that his bus might not have a trailer hitch. Seems like it should have one. But come to think of it, he really hasn't noticed one.

"I'm pretty sure it has one."

"Pretty sure? You don't know?"

"Well, we'll find out in a second."

Will pulls up next to AJ's bug, and they spill out. To AJ's delight and Will's chagrin, the bus is not equipped with a trailer hitch.

"Merely a minor setback," Will says.

"What are we gonna do now?"

"Drive into town and get Mr. Lockwood to put one on for us. A trailer hitch."

"That's gonna take forever."

"You seem to be forgetting, brother, that you're a vagrant now. The only home you have to go home to is the equivalent of a reform school grounding, meals slid under the crack of the door. You should be enjoying your freedom, not fretting over time. You see I have conquered time. It's always a weekend for me, brother."

"That's cause your old lady got you on her dole. My parents are liable to ship me off to some military academy in Tunisia if I drop out of school."

"If you're sixteen, they can't make you do anything."

"You sure about that?"

"Of course."

"Like you were sure about the trailer hitch."

"Shut up and get in. Mr. Peabody and I are off to get us a trailer hitch. You're welcome to join us if you like."

***

Frances Barrineau doesn't take teaching *Macbeth* for granted. She strives to do her best, to prepare each individual child for college English, both in refining writing skills and in having them glean vicarious experience from life lessons that great literature offers. She sees the play *Macbeth* as a brilliant embodiment of darkness, a warning that retreating inward is dangerous. When younger, she stressed in class Macbeth's stolid if unheroic response to the cruel trickery of the Weird Sisters' mummery—*at least we'll die with harness on our back*—but now she sees the play differently. Now, she stresses Macbeth's rapid degeneration, his sinking like Milton's Satan into ever-deepening abysses of hellishness. Surely, the way is not *the steep and thorny way to heaven* but somewhere in between the abyss and *the steep and thorny way*. It's time to bring the play to its end.

"So, tell me, Ollie. Do you feel cleansed? Purged of pity and terror?"

"No, Mrs. Barrineau," he says. "Perhaps catharsis depends somewhat on the spectacle of drama. Macbeth the man was less than awe-inspiring to me—at least that's my opinion after only reading the words on the page. If I saw the play, it might be different, but on the page, he's hard to pity. I pity Macduff, not Macbeth."

It's amazing, Fran thinks to herself, that they don't resent him, mock him. Maybe they do in other classes. A Yankee, our future valedictorian. Perhaps it's because he's the real alpha male of his class. The one who will make a mark in the world outside this town. Maybe they can sense it—the alpha maleness of him. Maybe it's biological.

"Thanks for saying what you believe, Ollie, instead of saying what you perhaps sense I wanted to hear. I, too, have not the visceral, drained awe I have at the end of *Lear*. As a tragic protagonist, the Thane of Glamis, the Thane of Cawdor lacks the profundity of soul of Othello and Hamlet. So, I say, good riddance, instead of 'what a piece of work is a man.'"

She closes her book, looks up, and smiles her crooked smile.

RIIIIIIINNNNNNNNNNNNNNNNNNNGGGGGGGG!!!

Activity Period

Activity Period: (10:35–10:50 A.M.)

As usual, Camilla Creel doesn't move from her seat when the bell rings for Activity Period. The rest of the girls in her home economics class can't wait to put away the dress patterns they're cutting out and stow those scissors so they can rush out into the teeming halls where boys cut fool and girls gossip. In Camilla's lap sits her purse—a large squarish cardboard contraption dressed in plastic stamped like snakeskin. A pink plastic brush matted with her orange hair sits inside along with a ragged gray change purse, which Camilla fetches and snaps open. They're still there— her two nickels—so she snaps shut the change purse, places it inside the larger purse, and clutches it again to her lap, her arms wrapped around it protectively. She'll sit here for five more minutes after Mrs. Matthews leaves to go to the lounge. Then she'll put away her pattern and scissors. Until then, she stares at the institutional clock to try to catch the minute hand moving.

It's unusual for Camilla to have spending money. In this case, she stealthily plucked ten pennies from a wishing fountain she found at the VA hospital where she had visited her great uncle Hiram, a recent amputee, the victim of diabetes. His wife Beulah had driven them to the hospital, located in North Charleston, about twenty miles from where Camilla stays. While Mama visited Uncle Hiram, Camilla sat out in the courtyard, because the odors of hospitals make her literally sick to her stomach. Out at the fountain when no one was looking, she lowered her hand into the cool water again and again until she had ten pennies, enough money for a Coca-Cola. Back home, she exchanged those pennies at Spell's Grocery for two nickels, rubbed them with her fingers, and dropped them in her change purse. She then proceeded past shelves loaded with Squirrel Nut Zippers, Tootsie Rolls, and Mary Janes, pushed open the screen door, and stepped into the dusk where a pair of bats zoomed and zigzagged in the purple light above the store.

Now the clock hand is in the right place, and the commotion outside Mrs. Matthews's open door has quieted into random lonely clunks, a distant locker door slamming, a far-off cry. Through the window she can see clumps of kids cavorting in bright sunshine. Camilla gets up, clutching her purse, and looking both ways as if crossing a street, she hesitantly steps out into the hall where a lone boy skedaddles down the stairs out of sight. The Coke machines are in the gym, and by now, she reckons the mad rush is about over. Walking slowly, she drops her books in her locker, figuring the longer it takes to get to the gym, the less likely she'll have to wait in line to buy her Coke. She and machines don't get along.

***

122

Josh Silverstein and Davis Bolster are engaged in a battle of hand slap. They stand facing one another, Josh's hands, pressed together as if in horizontal prayer and hovering just above his belt buckle, are wavering back and forth. Davis, his arms by his side, suddenly feigns with his right, then launches his left, slapping Josh's hands, left, right, left, right, – slap – slap – slap – then misses, the pyramid of Josh's red stinging hands arcing just out of reach of the sweep of Davis's palm. Now it's Josh's turn, his braces gleaming as he produces his patented diabolical grin.

***

Jill Birdsong has made her way to the Junior Civitan meeting in Miss McGee's room. The first project, selling Krispy Kreme doughnuts, netted over twenty-three dollars, which the club donated to the one-story sad-looking African American nursing home down the road from school. Jill is especially sensitive to the difficulties of the aged because her maternal grandfather, Granddaddy Chandler, is living at the Presbyterian Home in inconsolable widowerhood. She has come up with the idea that the club "adopt" a family from the nursing home to help them throughout the year with groceries, Christmas, and whatever. She thinks that connecting with a real family will be more meaningful than donating funds to the March of Dimes. Miss McGee considers it a "brilliant idea" so Jill is somewhat certain it will be approved.

In her early twenties, Miss McGee is what Jill's stepmother calls "perky." The kids adore her, so she'll be able to convince them to do whatever she wants, even though most of them would rather donate to the March of Dimes telethon so they can drive through downtown Charleston and over the Cooper River Bridges to deliver buckets of money to volunteers at Channel 2's studio. They might end up on TV along with firemen and disabled children. The other item on the agenda is what fundraiser they'll explore next. For a shy person like Jill, selling Krispy Kreme doughnuts is beyond no fun; it's something to dread. It takes an outgoing personality like Josh Silverstein, who sold something like forty-one boxes all by himself. She looks for but doesn't see Josh, though he was at the last meeting.

The room swarms with America's future leaders. For instance, ambitious Cathy Hawthorne, editor of the *Pine Needle*, wearing a plaid polyester pantsuit. Next to her stands her friend (and rival) Missy Roberts, President of the Junior Class, sporting a miniskirt flirting with above-the-knee illegality. Rozier Ravenel leans against the wall in white polo with white matching patent leather shoes next to Steve Murray in blue polo and khaki slacks. For some reason, girls' wearing pants terrifies the administration of SHS. Despite complaints from parents and students, girls can only wear pants on Mondays and Thursdays and only in conjunction with a matching top, the female equivalent of a man's dress suit. About the only hint of hipster fashion to be found in the room is a slight flare to pants legs and some below-the-ear sideburns sported by young men defying the dress code rule that sideburns should not extend beneath the middle of the ear. Miss McGee jokes with Danny Duncan who's shamelessly flirting with her. Jill, not fond of loud noises, is becoming increasingly uncomfortable as the din crescendos, but suddenly Danny Duncan, with his index and middle fingers in his mouth, blasts a startling, shrieking whistle that produces the desired effect – sudden silence.

"Folks," Miss McGee begins, "listen up. We got a lot on our plate today, so we better get going. I want to thank all of you who offered suggestions about our next fundraiser and what charity or charities will benefit. I've whittled down the suggestions to three, the three I deemed the most practicable, so now I'll present them, and we can debate, and hopefully come to a consensus."

***

Across campus outside the shop, the future tradesmen (and/or US infantrymen) of America mill around spitting and scratching their crotches. Their voices: deep Lowcountry brogues, long on vowels, short on vocabulary. Some of these boys are big, some of them scrawny. Most are good-natured fellows, like Goliath-sized Delbert Dawson, but others junk dog belligerents, like puny but sadistic Bucky Gaskins. The chip on Bucky's shoulder is sequoia sized. He might even be meaner than Bobbey Ray, but the thing is, as Bobbey Ray himself has pointed out, "Bucky's a scrawny little sumbitch."

"Hey, Bobbey," Lonnie Burbage calls, leaning against the metal shop building, "What was ol' man Carpenter yelling at you about?"

"He weren't yelling, bo. He was just telling me I best not jump no redheaded hippies and give them haircuts during football season."

Lonnie's a big boy with curly brown hair and a mouth that rarely if ever closes all the way. His teeth could use a good cleaning.

"That sure would be some fun, wouldn't it?"

"Damn right, bo."

"So you ain't gonna do it?"

"Dunno. I sure don't wanna get kicked off the team."

"I reckon there's no way you could disguise yourself with one of them bandit things tied around your face or pull a stocking over your head and jump that bitch without being recognized. Har har. That sure would be an improvement. I mean, a stocking over your face. Har-har."

Bobbey Ray, short and stocky, built like a bulldog, isn't amused. "You better shut that gotdam mouth of yours fore I smash you in your gotdam face."

"Take it easy, bo. I'm just cutting fool."

"It ain't funny."

Lonnie decides to forego any clever comebacks like "says who" because Bobbey Ray's temper is legendary. One night last summer over the course of four hours he punched for no apparent reason nine different people at the Water Wheel Swimming Pool. Later, he apologized, telling one of the victims, Eddie Droze, "Sorry, bo, but you know, liquor and beer just don't mix."

***

The Teachers' Lounge is a small dingy room with two saggy beige and brown plaid sofas, two oversized chairs, a blackboard, a telephone, a mimeograph machine, and a desk equipped with an electric typewriter. There's another adjoining tiny room with a telephone for privacy where Mrs. Matthews sits with the door closed speaking long distance trying to comfort her daughter, a junior at Converse College, whose boyfriend has just dumped her for one of her supposedly good friends. In the outer room on one of the sofas lounges Colonel Dukenfield who's fallen asleep with his mouth open, spittle practically bubbling from its corner. To the considerable consternation of Mrs. Laban, the Colonel has started to sort of snore – not really snore snore – but he's exhibiting the rhythmic beginnings, little gasps and snorts. Eula Lynne Laban does not frequent the lounge, but she was hoping to voice her dismay at the rapid deterioration of the school (the canary in the coal mine of civilization) as represented today in her encounters with Alex Jensen and Rusty Boykin. Unhappily for her, the only other teacher present in Quinn Burke, a Yankee and therefore a big part of the problem. When she walked past his class during her free period to see Principal Pushcart, it sounded as if the Battle of the Gettysburg was raging within.

"Looks like the Colonel might have had a late night," Quinn Burke says smiling.

If anything, Mrs. Laban's frown further furrows.

"Snort," snorts the Colonel.

Quinn wonders if he's actually awake and waits for some further comment, then picks up the sports section of the *The News and Courier*.

"Mr. Burke," Mrs. Laban says just when Quinn has managed to forget her rather formidable presence standing ramrod erect right next to him.

"Ma'am?" Even though Quinn was raised up in Vermont and didn't use "Ma'am" growing up, he's a quick study. He was using "y'all" within a week.

"Do you teach either Alex Jensen or Rusty Boykin?"

"No, Ma'am. Neither one."

"Do you know who they are?"

"I think so. One of them is redheaded, right? Always wearing that jacket with Mr. Zig Zag?"

Mrs. Laban cocks her head like a confused bird.

"Damn," Quinn thinks, "that was stupid, mentioning "Mr. Zig Zag." She'll ask me what it is, and I'll have to say an advertising trademark, and of course, she'll ask advertising what, and I'll fudge and say cigarettes, because if I say rolling papers, she'll wonder how I would know about such a thing."

Since there is thankfully no response from Mrs. Laban, Quinn asks, "What about them?"

"They've both been dismissed from school today."

"Oh yeah? What for?"

Eula Lynne recounts to Mr. Burke her take on the morning's events, the insubordination, the mockery of religion, their disgusting costumes. As Quinn politely listens, he's amazed that she so openly flaunts her violation of the laws of the land. He tries his best to look dismayed, but a part of him is finding her furor funny, and he's pretty sure that by now he's smirking, a habit his mother tried but failed to eliminate throughout his childhood. He's nodding his head as the screed continues. Quinn thinks to himself, "Last week you had a boy kill himself falling off a bridge, and she's all worked up about *hair below the collar* and the *frayed bottoms of dungarees*."

"Snort," snorts the Colonel as the door swishes open, and legendary Coach Schabel strides in, a good-looking man in his forties who resembles the actor Glenn Ford. Coach's face is creased from all those hours in the baking sun barking instructions, giving pep talks, but surprisingly, his coloring is grayish. Nevertheless, he displays the graceful movements of a younger man.

"Looks like the Colonel might have had a late night, last night," Coach says with a chuckle. "How you doing, Eula Lynne?"

"Sam, I was telling Mr. Burke here that I'm just beside myself with those two troublemakers Alex Jensen and Rusty Boykin."

"What have they done now?"

Quinn closes his eyes hoping against all hope.

"As I was telling young Mr. Burke just now, this morning in homeroom…"

***

Josh whacks Davis's hands, left, right, left, right, – slap – slap – slap – then whiffs, Davis's hands ducking just out of reach of the sweep of Josh's outstretched palm. Davis's turn: right, left, left, left, slap, slap, slap,

***

Camilla walks with her head down looking at the concrete, avoiding cracks, as she makes her way across campus to the gym. Throughout her entire trip, no one greets her, though she doesn't suffer any taunts. She counts four concrete cracks, then looks up, the door to the gym four cracks closer now, then looks down, counts four cracks, and looks up again. When she looks up the last time, there's no one at the red Coke machine in the corner, so she quickens her steps. Once at the machine, she fumblingly opens her pocketbook to retrieve the change purse but seems at a loss as what to do with the larger pocketbook. After a moment of hesitation, she places the pocketbook on the green rubber mat next to the vending machine. Oh no, now a boy's walking up behind her, so she fumbles opening the change purse, and, yes, the nickels are still there, so she takes one out, her weathered hand shakingly guiding it to the slot. Kerplunk, it falls all the way through the machine to the change chute. She does the same with the sister nickel, and kerplunk, it too falls all the way through to the change chute. Nevertheless, she mashes the Coke button, but, of course, no Coke appears. She mashes it again and again, tears arising in her eyes.

"Excuse me," the boy behind her says, "but the coins didn't engage."

"Huh?"

"The coins didn't engage. This machine doesn't like nickels."

It's a voice from up north. The boy's wearing granny glasses.

He reaches into the coin chute and retrieves the nickels. Camilla is terrified, afraid that he's stealing her money. He puts in the first nickel, then smacks the machine on the side. Clink. Again. Rattle. Bang. Clink. "Okay," he says, "press the button you want."

Slowly, Camilla extends her trembling hand and mashes the Coke button, and the machine groans, and she can hear the can sliding down through the flap door.

"There you go," the boy says.

"Thank you, Sir," Camilla says, her free hand covering her mouth, then walks away quickly.

"*Sir*?" Ollie can't believe it. "She called me sir!"

***

Miss McGee, as Jill predicted, has convinced the crew to "adopt a family" at what they call the Colored Home; unfortunately, however, she mentioned Jill as the "sponsor" of the idea, which embarrasses Jill, who prefers anonymity. Cindy Cauthen wanted to donate the money to the March of Dime Telethon, essentially because she wants as much exposure as humanly possible. Cindy is a goal-oriented person who color codes her notebooks and whose most important quest is getting into a prestigious university. If not an Ivy League institution, then something on the order of Vanderbilt or Emory. If she could be telecast delivering money to Channel 2 anchorman Carroll Conroy, it could be very advantageous. Unfortunately, Miss McGee brought up "the fact" (as she called it) that much of the money donated to entities like the March of Dimes goes to overheads and salaries, and that wouldn't be true at the Colored Home. Every "red cent" would go to the family, and though no doubt the March of Dimes does its share of good, you wouldn't get the "real satisfaction of being able to experience firsthand the fruits of our good works."

"Yes, Danny," she says acknowledging Mr. Duncan's raised left hand.

"I agree with you, Miss M. Those people at the March of Dimes spend a lot of their money on superfluous things like water coolers."

"That's it," sighs Cindy among the approving chuckles. The show of hands confirms her fears.

"Now, then," Miss McGee says. "Let's discuss how we're going to raise the money to perform these good deeds."

***

Davis whacks Josh's hands, left, right, left, right, – slap – slap – slap – then misses, Josh's hands jerking just out of reach of the sweep of Davis's outstretched palm. Josh's turn: right, left, left, left, slap, slap, slap.

***

Eula Lynne seems to have a sympathetic audience in Sam Schabel. Rather than nodding his head mechanically like a Parkinson's victim (i.e., like Quinn Burke), Coach Schabel is commenting on her complaints. He attributes the breakdown of traditional morality to liberal college professors, Hollywood, and the influx of liberal Yankees, but most of all, he blames permissive parenting.

"Snort," snorts the Colonel.

"And that music," Mrs. Laban says, "if I had been blessed with a child and I ever heard him or her listening to that jungle music, you better believe there would be consequences. You're right, Sam. I mean about the parenting. I agree with you about the permissive parents. No child reared in my home would ever want to listen to that kind of music because Joe and I would provide the type of nurture and Christian upbringing that inoculates youngsters from such barbarism."

"Snort," snorts the Colonel.

"Well, young Mr. Burke," Coach Schabel says, "you're being mighty quiet over there. Do you have any insights to share? After all, you're a young person yourself."

"And an invading Northerner as well, don't forget."

Nervous, awkward smiles.

"I dunno," Quinn continues, "about parents being able to shield their kids from the influences of popular culture. So, Mrs. Laban, you don't have any kids?"

"No, we've not been blessed with children."

"In my last ed. class up at Burlington, I ran across this statistic that suggested that something like 88 or 90 percent – something astronomical – of kids are more influenced by their peers than their parents."

Coach Schabel makes a theatrical production of glancing at his watch. "I wish," he says, "I had time to continue this fascinating discussion, but as they say, I got some fish to fry."

He gently puts his hand on Mrs. Laban's arm. He suspects that she was a good-looking woman in her day, albeit an unimpregnable fortress. "Eula Lynne, I hope you have a wonderful day. So long, Quinn. You take it easy. And a bit of advice, young man: don't believe everything you read."

"Sure thing, Coach."

As Sam Schabel leaves, Eula Lynne steps back to glance in the adjoining room where Vicky Matthews continues in hushed tones to try to comfort her daughter.

"Well, Mr. Burke," Eula Lynne says, "Goodbye. And. Please accept my apology if I've offended you."

"Offended me? How?"

"You know, about those things I said about Northerners."

Quinn offers a genuine, good-natured smile. "I'm pretty used to that by now," he says. "No offense taken. Have a nice day."

As Eula Lynne turns to leave, the Colonel blurts, talking in his sleep, "Cakes and ales."

Eula Lynne momentarily stops to see if he's addressing her. She looks down at the human wreck of the Colonel, spittle bubbling from the corner of his mouth.

The Colonel: "Cakes and ales!"

Looking at Mr. Burke, she shakes her head and takes her leave.

***

Safely seated on a bench alone, Camilla savors every sip of her Coca Cola. She hopes that someone will see her drinking it, looking like a regular girl. From across the way, she spots her favorite teacher Mrs. Laban walking across the quad back toward the main building. It's unusual to see Mrs. Laban out-of-doors, but she walks the same way outside as in, like you could stack a mess of bricks on her head and they wouldn't fall off.

***

As Miss McGee brings the Junior Civitan meeting to its close, restive inattention rustles. Students twitter, whisper, fiddle with book satchels and purses.

"Listen up. We're not quite done. So, here's the scoop. Jill, I'm putting you in charge of selecting a family to 'adopt,' and Nanci, I'm putting you in charge of the bake sale. That said, I'm officially calling this meeting to a close."

Slap, whiff, slap, slap. Whoosh. Slap. Whiff. Slap, whap, whap, whiff.

Art Room, Maggie Blackthorne: "Althea, the bell's about to ring,"

Outside the shop, Bucky Gaskins: "Bo, the bell's fixin' to ring for Break to be over."

Inside, Josh Silverstein's locker: a poem by Edgar Allen Poe.

RIIIIIIIIIIIIIIIIIIIIIIIIIINNNNNNNNNNNGGGGGGGG !!!

Fourth Period

Between Activity Period and Class (10:50–10:55 A.M.)

When Eula Lynne Laban returns to her classroom, several students are standing around George, the anatomical dummy, double-checking the locations of his color-coded pancreas and gall bladder. As she enters, heels clacking, she manages a chirpy *good morning*, but she's feeling down in the dumps about those ungracious comments regarding Yankees she voiced in front of Quinn Burke a moment ago. What if the situation had been reversed, if she had been a first-year teacher starting off in a strange, exotic Northern city like, say, Bloomingdale, Indiana, and two of her older colleagues started generalizing about Southerners the way she and Sam had about Northerners? No, she wouldn't like that one little bit. "Some Yankees'—not all of them, mind you—pushy ways can be obnoxious," Sam said back yonder. "For one thing," he had complained, "some of them don't acknowledge the difference between adults and children, which they call 'kids.' Their children say 'yeah' instead of 'yes sir' or 'yes ma'am' and are impertinent in general." With Quinn sitting right there flipping through the paper, Eula Lynne followed up Coach's complaints with specific examples, like that McKell boy saying "so what" when she informed him that the back end of his shirttail had come untucked. She had never in all her life been so disrespectfully treated. Bad habits, she noted to Coach, are harder to break than good habits are to pick up. Coach Sam chuckled and said that statement needed to be rendered in needlepoint, framed, and hung in every den in America. As Eula Lynne softened her face with a smile, he nodded to Quinn and got the hell out of Dodge. Once out of the door, he strode toward the gym, the incident already having evaporated into oblivion as Xs and Os formulated in his mind's mist.

On the bright side, Quinn Burke didn't seem at all offended, but how couldn't he be? Why *isn't* he? Then it dawns upon her: That overgrown pipsqueak isn't offended because he thinks he's *better than we are*. He looks at us and sees *Hee-Haw*, Cousin Minnie Pearl. Eula Lynne decides not to follow up her oral apology with a more formal written one. Her sincerely spoken words should suffice. Anyway, now's not the time for self-recrimination. She has a Biology II mid-term exam to administer.

Even though it's four minutes until the second bell, Eula Lynne politely shoos the students to their desks, because "this examination should take the entire period, and when the green flag of the second bell goes down, I want y'all to start racing." NASCAR isn't all that popular with the college prep crowd, but her husband Joe is a huge fan and listens to the big races, like Daytona, on the radio when these events preempt regularly scheduled broadcasts of Braves baseball. Students are continuing to file in, so she retrieves her black-green spiralbound gradebook and opens it to 4th Period. There these students' carefully formed, alphabetized surnames appear in black Indian ink among grids of color-coded Arabic numerals.

If this were a regular class and not a test, she would call each child's name out loud, because she feels it is important for each student to hear his name spoken at least once a day during a class. However, to save time, she's glancing over those half-moon reading glasses to identify students and then peering down through the lenses to the box next to their names in her gradebook. Tick tick tick. For a regular class, she would place marks (an x in this case) next to students' names who were absent; however, because this is a test—in fact, a midterm examination—she ticks the students who are present and leaves an incriminating blank next to students' names who are absent. Missing a Laban test is a big deal. You need a doctor's excuse. She has only two sections of Biology II, and she always makes out two different tests, an A and a B version, so cheating becomes more difficult. She's proud that students respect her wishes about test attendance, and it's very rare for her to have to compose a make-up (which Jonas Salk and Dr. Christiaan Bernard might have trouble passing).

The checkmarks increase: Becky Baldwin, Mike Bragg, Dave Hiatt, Sharon Mallard. Then she notices Rusty's name and tiptoes and leans to peer over Dave Hiatt's shoulder, but that's Eric Hutchinson, a different redhead. Taking out her impressive ring of keys, she locates the smallest one, the one for her cabinet, unlocks its aluminum door, and procures the stack of mimeographed Biology II midterms. After carefully placing the stack on her desk, she returns to the cabinet and locks it. Mrs. Laban believes it's important to be a role model, so she makes a point of doing everything in a deliberate manner to embody, as it were, her inner organization with an outward show of methodical movement. Of course, none of the students are paying her a bit of attention as they shuffle homemade flashcards and flip through their spiral composition books.

"It appears that we're all here except Rusty and Alex, so I'm going to distribute the examinations face down. Of course, y'all know by now that you're not to turn them over before I give my say-so."

Rather than passing them back, she walks past each desk and places the five-pager face down as she conducts reconnaissance, keeping a sharp eye out for telltale signs of cheating: open notebooks in bins underneath the desks, writing on wrists, trembling hands. Once all the tests are distributed, she returns to her desk and once again consults her timepiece. There are still two minutes left, and Eric Hutchinson's drumming his pencil on his desk like some kind of hyperactive Ginger Baker. Mrs. Laban strides over to him—click clack, click clack—and puts her blue-veined hand on his. The drumming ceases, and Steve Murray glows a snickering bright red as he glances over to Mike Bragg, who grins back in appreciation. Poor Eric looks as if he's just swallowed a peeled lemon, as if being touched by Mrs. Laban might make him radioactive.

***

Across the hall in Mrs. Middleton's honors chemistry class, the talented science and math crew sit two to a table with their lab partners. At the beginning of the year, Rozier

Ravenel pragmatically chose Ollie Wyborn as his partner, much to the chagrin of Cindy Cauthen. Jill is teamed with her good friend and neighbor Kathi Haley, who, like Jill, is also in Beta Club and, who, like Jill, is also a National Honor Society shoo-in.

Cindy Cauthern could kick herself for letting that jerk Rozier co-opt her heartthrob at the beginning of the year. Both she and Rozier were co-chairs of the new student welcoming committee, and it became evident even before classes started that Ollie was a super student. He shared his dreams about becoming an astronaut, and if there is anyone on this campus who has the talents necessary to be tapped by NASA as an astronaut, it's Ollie.

Imagine being married to an astronaut! The framed picture on the buffet: uniformed Ollie, perhaps graying around the temples, Cindy in her pristine prime next to him, their two darling daughters, Paulette and Chisholm (her mother's maiden name) in front in their pink ruffled Easter dresses. Of course, Rozier chose Ollie simply for utilitarian reasons: easy As on all of his labs. In theory, the partners are to "work together," to "collaborate," etc., the division of labor supposedly more or less equal.

Yeah, right.

For his part, Ollie can't seem to keep from letting his eyes wander over to the back of Jill Birdsong's head, the lightly frosted hair that flips under just below her collar. He hates the fact that somehow some sort of chemical or metabolic adolescence-triggered hormonal process is short-circuiting his rationality. Staring at the back of Jill's head is stupid. Ineffectual. Most probably counter-productive. What if she turns around and perceives that he was staring at her? He chides himself for being so cowardly. Imagine, he's actually been hatching a dishonest ruse about the poet John Donne to initiate a personal relationship under false pretenses. The longer he waits to ask her, the more likely it will be that she already will have a date. And what if she does? It doesn't mean that she doesn't like him, that she won't be flattered, that she won't go out with him in the future. What's there to lose? Just ask her, ask her, ask her…

"Snap out of it, man," Rozier whispers. "Looks like you're slipping into a coma."

Ollie weakly chuckles. "I guess I'm preoccupied."

RIIIIIIIIINNNNNNNNNNNGGGGGGGGGG!

Fourth Period (10:55–11:40)

Dave Hiatt, a savvy test taker, is flipping through Mrs. Laban's exam, getting "the lay of the land."

Use the diagram below and your knowledge of the living environment to answer questions 20 through 22, which follow.

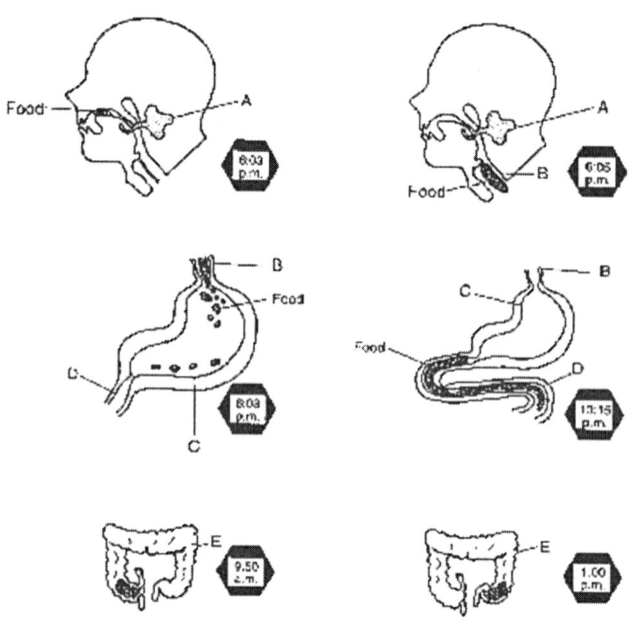

20. The diagrams above illustrate the pathway and the time frame for the digestion of a wholesome serving of a certain biology teacher's celebrated dish, Meatloaf Spectacular, which consists of ground beef, ketchup, salt, pepper, diced Vidalia onions, and whole wheat breadcrumbs. During which time period does most of the digestive action of bile and pancreatic juice occur?

a. 6:03 p.m. to 6:05 p.m.   c. 10:15 p.m. to 9:50 a.m.

b. 6:05 p.m. to 6:08 p.m.   d. 9:50 a.m. to 1:00 p.m.

21. The diagrams illustrate the pathway and the time frame for the digestion of mouthwatering Meatloaf Spectacular, consisting of ground beef, ketchup, diced

onions and whole-wheat breadcrumbs. Chemical digestion of the breadcrumbs begins after hydrolytic enzymes are secreted by structure.

(a.) A (b.) B (c.) C (d.) D

23. Which foods should be included in a balanced diet as a good source of roughage?

(a.) fried chicken and mashed potatoes (b.) watermelon and cantaloupe (c.) scrambled eggs (d.) boiled peanut shells

22. The diagrams illustrate the pathway and the time frame for the digestion of scrumptious Meatloaf Spectacular. An irritant can cause erosion in the lining of structure C. leading to a disorder known as

(a.) appendicitis (b.) ulcer (c.) constipation (d.) colon cancer (e.) diarrhea

Piece of cake!

***

Having successfully negotiated the sparsely traveled roads of the outskirts of Summerville, South Carolina, then through the heart of the town, Will Waring and Alex Jensen are standing at the checkout counter of Mueller's Hardware Store, Will with a trailer hitch and his mother's checkbook in his hands. The store is dimly lit and smells, not surprisingly, like a hardware store. In AJ's semi-stoned state, the everyday tools of Man on display—hammers, saws, crescent wrenches—have taken on a simple grandeur. Even the heaps of nails in bins seem somehow beautiful. He, of course, is about as handy as a skink, has about as much common sense as Soupy Sales. The only thing he's ever made, a Pinewood Derby Cub racer, looked as if it had been hacked into shape by a hatchet. Outside in the VW bus, Mr. Peabody (aka Hambone) is doing his patented impersonation of a victim of the Spanish Inquisition. As pedestrian Mildred Smith strolls by and hears the horrid commotion, the familiar face of Satan-eyed Charlie Manson flickers across the drive-in movie screen of her mind. She would call a policeman if there were one present, but officer Dickey is several blocks away stiffly rising from his stool at the poolhall and saluting goodbye to Buzz (officer Applegate's cruiser is safely stowed in Mrs. Ronald Richland's garage for the duration of a quickie). As Dickey waddles toward the door, the handcuffs, billy club and gun dangle like talismans, jangling with his heavy steps. He shoots a suspicious glance at Eddie Jenrette and Hank Pritchard who, infuriatingly, pay him not a nanosecond of nervous attention.

***

Although he wasn't raised a guilt-ridden Catholic, Rusty didn't fully enjoy his first intercourse, a sexual encounter, mind you, that involved "the girl of his dreams," a coupling whose odds of occurring were as likely as drawing thirteen consecutive royal straight flushes. If you had asked him this morning when his mother Ginny roused him from bed, what would he give for the chance to consummate his love for Sandy Welch, he might have said, "My left testicle plus twenty-points of IQ." And yet, a few minutes ago, there he was staring into the milky reflection of Will's bathroom mirror, Sandy standing behind him, scissors in her left hand, yanking a brush through his tangled hair, then running a comb, then clipping the ends in little deft castanet-like snip snip snips. There were those unexpected and unsettling touches, a caressing clasp of his towel-draped shoulder as she tilted her own head back to sway her glorious hair like a swinging pendulum. After her "ta-da," Rusty stood up, peering in the mirror, halfheartedly complimenting her on the hair cut (but thinking it might be too short). Then she raked her fingers through his hair, and it sprang back, like magic almost, to its former length. When she saw his huge grin, she put her arms around his neck and hugged him from behind, and not even thinking, he turned around and started kissing her.

She was like no girl he had ever encountered before, aggressive with her tongue. They groped their way to Will's sofa and plopped down. Unfortunately, Rusty's cerebrum kicked in with the fear that Will Waring could come busting through the door, bringing to a screeching halt the frenzied groping Rusty couldn't fully enjoy now because he was thinking that Will Waring would show up at any minute. When he realized that her hand was clasping his butt, he became more aggressive, and Sandy began to unbutton her blouse – and Rusty thought, *Please, please, please, Will, please be driving in the opposite direction toward Nome, Alaska, please, please, please.* And even though he didn't know what to do, she helped him, and as soon as they were "doing it" (in SHS polite girl parlance), he thought to himself, *Oh, this feels so good, but I gotta stop, yes, I gotta stop, feels good, gotta stop, feels so good, gotta stop, man, this feels good, gotta stop, gotta stop, ought to stop, gotta stop, time to stop, I need to stop.* But then it was too late to stop—it was happening—the fireworks—and he pictured millions and millions and millions of microscopic sperm cells wiggling their way on their quest, way beyond his control now, with their own life-or-death agenda, and he thought to himself, *Oh shit.*

***

Mrs. Middleton, the chemistry teacher, has done the unexpected. She's completely reassigned lab partners, having the boys in the class draw a girl's name out of a SHS football helmet she keeps in the classroom as a talisman/decoration. Mrs. Middleton is the type of teacher who tolerates whining, and Rozier Ravenel is doing so *a voce alta* in his blueblood brogue: "But Mizz Middleton, Ollie and I work so well together. We've become a team. Like, um, Lewis and Clark, discovering new vistas of chemical reactions."

Ollie, of course, would like nothing better than to go coed with lab partners (even though he knows the odds with ten boys and ten girls are, of course, 10 to 1, thus rendering the desired pairing of Jill and himself unlikely). But then again, what are the odds of having a perfectly balanced class as far as gender goes? Drawing Jill *is* a possibility, so he wishes Rozier would cease his self-interested rant so they could begin the process. Oh, man, it would be so cool. So fortuitous. Of course, Rozier's whining won't work. Ollie conjectures (correctly) that Mrs. Middleton wants to compare the quality of these new partners' lab reports with those reports written by the original pairings. Perhaps she suspects some cheating's going on or that one or the other partner is doing more than his or her share. After all, it's midterm: time to shake things up. Ollie has tried to have Rozier do his fair share, has assigned him specific duties, but for Ollie it's easier, less problematic, to bear most of the burden himself than it is to rely on unreliable Rozier. It's embarrassing to have to point out Rozier's scientific errors, to suggest alternate wordings for his haywire syntax, and to discover those dizzying shifts in verb tense Rozier's prone to commit.

Jill, for her part, agrees with Rozier. She and Kathi have a very effective partnership whose division of labor is ideal. There are a couple of cute boys she wouldn't mind being partners with—like Rozier and Rick Hahn—but it would be awkward. Or maybe she might get Ollie Wyborn, who's a very nice guy, if a bit too serious, and with a very high voice for a boy. He's sort of been looking at her funny lately. Getting Ollie might be intimidating, though. He's downright brilliant—if not a genius—so he might not like having a partner who's not quite on his level. Then again, Rozier's not exactly on Ollie's level (understatement of the year), and he certainly sees his partnership with Ollie to be a worthwhile set-up. "Rozier," she thinks to herself, "Shut up all right all ready."

Finally, Mrs. Middleton snaps, "Okay now, Rozier, that's enough. I'm running out of patience. I've cut out the names, they're here in the helmet, so here, Rozier, draw first."

"Oh, Mizz, Middleton."

"I mean it."

"Okay, okay," he says, reaching into the helmet and retrieving the folded paper. As the helmet is passed to Rick

Hahn, Rozier opens the paper and sees he's drawn Jill Birdsong. He smiles. The brainy female equivalent of Ollie!

When the helmet gets to Ollie, only four pieces of paper are left, and he wishes he could have gone first when all possibilities were relevant. Unlike others, who peeked inside and rummaged around, Ollie reaches in and plucks the first one he touches. As he unfolds it, he sees the first letter – C. As randomness would have it, his lab partner will be Cindy Cauthen.

***

Officer Dickey has a hunch. It wouldn't surprise him a gotdam bit if that missing girl weren't holed up at the Jenrette's plantation. He'd be willing to bet his WWII vintage Lugar that he could find him some of that whacky tobacky out there. Find the shit, call in a warrant, bust them bluebloods, get some headlines in the *Summerville Scene/Journal.* Might be a pill or two laying 'round there that he could use himself. Why not? It's a nice little drive that way, and it takes him right past Bacons Bridge, so he could do a little surveillance while he's at it. As he struggles out of the poolhall door toward his cruiser, he sees a hippie van headed south on Main and a left arm pointing straight out of the window signaling a turn as the vehicle slows to pull into Lockwood's Esso. A bright yellow El Camino shoots by, speeding in the other direction, blasting a muffler-less roar. Ignoring the El Camino, Dickey stops walking to watch the two boys clamber out of the hippie van. One's a longhair, and the other boy's got something silver in his hand. Officer Dickey decides to mosey down

148

there to see why they're not in school and if they know anything about a red Mustang.

"So, Mr. Lockwood. You say it'll be an hour?"

"At least that long. I got an oil change to do before I can get to it."

"Okay, then. I guess we'll walk down and get a hot dog and come back. Thanks, Mr. Lockwood."

"Sure thing, Will."

"Just don't stand there, AJ. Hand him the hitch."

"Oh yeah. Sorry. Here."

"YYYYYYYYYOOOOOOOOOWLLLLLLLLLL!!!"

Mr. Lockwood drops the hitch, its bouncing on the pavement making metallic music as he foots a little jig in fear of his feet. "Good God, what the hell is that?"

"That's Mr. Peabody," Will says, picking up the hitch, "our basset hound."

"I tell you what, Will. Take that gotdang dog home and come back. I ain't working on that bus with that critter in there."

"He won't hurt you. He can't get out."

"I don't care. I just as soon not hear that howling. Sounds like he's shitting a hippopotamus or something."

"Hey," AJ says. "That's pretty good, Mr. Lockwood."

Will glances to his right. "Uh-oh," he says under his breath as Dickey turns from the sidewalk and starts to approach them.

What AJ sees is a walrus in a uniform waddling toward him.

"Why, hello, Officer Dickey," Mr. Lockwood says. "What can I do for you?"

"I'd like to ask these boys a couple of questions."

"Go right ahead," Mr. Lockwood says as if he's their daddy, as if you need permission to ask his customers questions.

"Why ain't you boys in school?"

"I'm a dropout," Will says.

"How old are you, boy?"

"I'll be 18 in April. We're both the same age," Will replies.

"Who 'round here drives a red Mustang?"

Perhaps because his father's a lawyer, AJ doesn't fear policemen, the way Will and Rusty do. "In all due respect, sir," he says, "the county highway department should be able to help you there."

"You trying to be smart, boy?"

AJ holds his hands up with his palms toward Dickey. "No, honest, sir. Just trying to help. I don't know of anybody that drives a red Mustang. Will, do you know anybody who drives a red Mustang?"

"I don't know of any."

Dickey turns to Mr. Lockwood, "John, do you know of anyone who drives a red Mustang?"

"I've seen a red Mustang, but for all I know, there's more than one. I certainly don't recall servicing a red Mustang."

***

Although Rusty had confidently announced his agnosticism to his soon-to-be-lover some fifty-five minutes ago, he hasn't absolutely abandoned belief in a fair-minded Deity, especially when he's in trouble. Ideally, this deity would be a Father God, the Cosmic Equivalent of Ward Clever, cleanshaven, fair, loving all creatures great and small. Jesus, of course, is Love Personified, but He's obviously not in charge. Oh, how comforting it would be to know with confidence that your prayer would be heard:

Daddy God, I been a bad boy. Slothful.

I'm going to fail Anatomy. I deserve to. That's okay.

I've been lustful, but as You know as Omniscient Everything. It was not premeditation. Natural Selection made me do it!

Please, please, please, stop those sperm.
Please, please, please, no ovum, please.
I'll never do it again without protection.
I swear by all the holy fools.

Of course, some attribute the lawyerly "acts of God"—famine in Bangladesh, lightning striking a golfer—to the Deity's working in mysterious ways. Maybe this lovemaking happening just now was God-ordained so that the offspring of the union might become a great man—a Lincoln or Churchill—who in the future would save democracy and freedom of religion, despite the wrenching changes the pregnancy would engender in little Rusty's and little Sandy's little lives, analogous drops of H(OH) in a mighty cosmic ocean multiplied by all the galaxies to the tenth power. That's how insignificant he and everybody else is. But then again, odds are just as good as that the union might produce Richard Speck or Lee Harvey Oswald. The most likely outcome, though, would be of the baby ending up a mediocre blending of X and Y chromosomes, a future Wally Cox or Lumpy Rutherford. But Rusty knows thinking like this is fruitless; either she's pregnant or not, either there's a God or not. He looks up at the clock on the mantle: five past XI. The only thing for certain is that Mrs. Laban is going to put a little black circle in the gradebook for his mid-term exam grade, and that means his father's going to go apeshit.

While Rusty engages in his dark musings, Sandy's eyes are closed, her head in his lap on the sagging green sofa, their love nest, a little smile on her perfect little mouth, the record jackets strewn about, the Valium kicking in quite nicely, thank you. Now she wishes that she had done it with Tradd, even if he were so full of himself, because then he could be the dad or Tripp could be the dad or now Rusty could be the dad, or maybe her period will come after all, or maybe it's a hysterical pregnancy (she's been reading up), but now, it's time to rest her eyes and just lie there watching the blobs of color floating between her closed eyelids and her brain.

It, in fact, occurred to Rusty after his sexual debut that his idealized vision of Sandy and what just happened didn't exactly jive. Rusty's conception of Love comes from books (*Romeo and Juliet* and *The Count of Monte Cristo* and *Cyrano de Bergerac)*. Surely, Sandy's done it with Tripp and perhaps others before him up North. Or maybe she hasn't. Maybe, in her grief, or maybe—no, she was in charge, in heat, an expert, and not quiet while it was happening. And now as this occurs to him again, he's flooded with jealousy—jealousy for a dead boy and for everyone out there who might steal her away from him, and he's glad she's asleep because he might be starting to cry. Oh man, this isn't Shit Creek he's up without a paddle, but Shit Styx, Shit Acheron, and Shit Lethe all rolled into one gargantuan sewer of potential doom.

* * *

Ollie Wyborn isn't an admirer of Rozier Ravenel. He senses in Rozier an aura of superiority based, as far as Ollie can tell, on the mere fact that his last name is spelled R-a-v-e-n-e-l. This sense of entitlement based on bloodlines strikes Ollie as absurd. It doesn't matter to Ollie whether he can trace his ancestry to Eric the Red or Thorkel the Comic Sidekick. What matters is what comes from within, what one accomplishes. Ollie has staked out the lab table right next to Jill, though Rozier stands literally between him and her. Already, Cindy Cauthen, who has make-up caked on as thick as Buster Keaton, is violating Ollie's personal space. He can detect her blemishes, little hillocks, beneath the pasty compound composing the camouflage.

* * *

Now that the throaty engine of the VW bus is blaring through its well-rusted muffler, Alex and Will are smiling world championship smiles. There they were stoned and maintaining in front of the PO-lice. Even Hambone/Peabody is happy to see them, his docked tail

153

wagging like a metronome gone haywire. What better way to celebrate than take Mr. Peabody home, smoke another joint, return to Mr. Lockwood, and cruise down for lunch at the poolhall. The day's young. It's not even noon. Those poor fools in school still got four hours of hoop jumping to go, according to Will's lazy reckoning. The 8-Track engages, and, of course, it's Hendrix, just in the first verse of "Are You Experienced?"

"That was great, man," Will says, then impersonates AJ. "In all due respect, sir, the county highway department should be able to help you there."

AJ singing along, "Well, I am."

Will joins in, "Are you experienced?"

Jimi answers, "Well, I am."

"I wonder why neither one of us told him that Sandy drives a red Mustang," AJ says. "You'd think your instinct would tell you, especially if you were stoned, to go ahead and truthfully answer a cop's questions, doesn't it?"

"Speak for your own instinct, man. My instinct tells me that when you're talking to the cops, you say as little as possible."

AJ switches to his cartoon Sherman voice. "Mr. Peabody, we'll feed you some lunch and water when we get to Will's house, and then we'll set the Way Back Machine to ancient Rome for a Bacchanalian night out."

"Well, listen to you," Will says. "Forgotten all about your schoolessness, haven't you?"

"Dammit, Will! I had all but forgotten! You bastard! (Theatrically a la Boris Karloff): Ohhhhhhhhh Gawwwdddd. It's upon me again. The fit's upon me again."

YYYYYYYYOOOOOOOOOWLLLLLLLLLL…

AJ turns around to pet Mr. Peabody. "Calm thyself, canine. We gonna be back at Will's cat kennel in no time. I certainly hope that during your travels you've acquired a taste for Purina Cat Chow. Or better yet, calico."

"Changing the subject, AJ. If you could screw any girl in this town, who would it be?"

"What kind of waste of time question is that?"

"No harm in dreaming. Who would it be?"

"I dunno."

"Come on, man."

"Who would you? That's why you asked me. You don't care what my answer is, you just want to tell me your dream chick. Go ahead. I'm dying to know."

"Why so touchy, man?"

"I'm not touchy. Who is it?"

"Never mind, man, never mind."

***

The new arrangement of Mrs. Middleton's young scientists has raised the hormone level in the lab past the redline pheromone danger zone. Cindy Cauthen is stretching and yawning next to a somewhat disheartened Ollie Wyborn. Jill Birdsong finds herself on edge in a rather pleasant way; her erstwhile partner, Kathi Haley, is wed, so to speak, to Mitch Mitchum, a nice enough fellow, but let's face it, the antithesis of Bobby Sherman. Mrs. Middleton herself seems more enthusiastic than normal, energetically outlining today's lab, an experiment in which the students will mix a solid and a liquid to create a gas.

One of Mindy Middleton's recurring nightmares is a chemistry lab that ends in conflagration. Sometimes, in all-too-frequent dreams, she's overslept and is rushing in slow motion to a classroom where students have taken matters into their own combustible hands, or worse (at least more frustratingly), she can't find her room, the halls of SHS having mutated into an exhaustively intricate Escher maze. However, in the worst dream of all, she has forgotten that she has a chemistry class until just now; it's halfway through the year, weeks and months of neglect have passed – all her fault – and as she pushes open the door of the lab, she discovers to her horror that her little chemists have mutated into hideous creatures, monsters – *Planet of the Apes*!

"People," she's saying, "I can't stress enough how important it is to wear your goggles at all times and to work only in the hood. The chemicals we're employing in this experiment can be dangerous. Poisonous. We need to employ extreme caution, but I know you will, because you're a very mature congregation of eleventh graders!"

Rozier Ravenel's paying about as much attention to Mrs. Middleton's admonitions as he is to the escalating tensions in Canada between Pierre Trudeau's government and *Front de libération du Québec*. Instead, Rozier's imagining intercepting a pass and streaking (an impossibility) down the sidelines 99 yards for the winning T.D. in the upcoming game versus archrival Berkeley High. The crowd is on their feet, the cheers deafening, and Aphrodite-like cheerleader Shelia Smith's heart is melting like a half-gallon of Bordon's butter pecan ice cream. Rozier doesn't need to pay attention anyway. Jill Birdsong will carry him through this lab, the way Ollie would have if he had been his partner.

"Okay, class. The solid we're using is ferrous sulfide. Who knows the symbol for ferrous sulfide? Kathi?"

"Itn't it *Fe* for iron and *S* of sulfur?"

"Good," Mrs. Middleton says, emphatically writing *FeS* on the board behind her. "So, let's get out our goggles and make sure we're under the hoods. I want to see goggles on every single student. Like I said, these chemicals are combustible, so we're going to need to pay close attention."

***

For scheduling reasons, the Shop and Ag boys all have 5A lunch as opposed to 5B lunch. Mr. Carpenter, after all, needs to eat, and eating just happens to be his hobby. Fried foods are his favorite: fried shrimp, fried hushpuppies, fried okra, fried green tomatoes. No way are these bucks going to be left unsupervised with this vast armory of potential weapons: saws, screwdrivers, hammers, wrenches, not to mention electric staplers and power saws. A couple of the boys are biracial, known as *Summerville Indians,* and being called *yellow* is a *good damn way to get your ass cut, bo.* Bobbey Ray Bosheen's construction team, which consists of Sonny Kirven, Donnie Dickson, Bucky Gaskins, and Arthur T. Hall, is framing a storage shed, and you couldn't ask for much better weather—the temperature having risen to about 68 sunny degrees. Arthur T. owns a transistor radio,

157

which is blasting George Jones's "It's Been a Good Year for the Roses" underneath the rat-a-tat of hand-driven nails.

The boys are framing the walls using the x method; that is, they're hammering the 2x4s flat on the platform, then raising the wall up from the concrete floor to stand straight up. Arthur T. is the foreman of this project because he knows what he's doing from the real world of summer labor, and the boys respect him. It helps that he's twenty years old and has been shaving since he was eleven. Arthur T. *don't* take *no shit* from *nobody* and could *whup* anyone's ass in his crew, including Bobbey Ray's. Not only that but Arthur T. sports the *bodaciousest* haircut: parted on both sides and combed down into an arrowhead-like point just below his hairline. Unfortunately, Arthur T. is too old to play football, his last year of eligibility having been 1969. If he'd had practice this afternoon, he might not be working the boys so hard, but then again, as foreman, he's not the one driving those nails. The reason he's still in high school is that he promised his beloved Me-Maw that *yes ma'am I swear I'll finish school* as she lay in bed skinny as a skeleton and racked with coughs, dying of lung cancer.

Bobbey Ray's hankering for a break, hankering to be the Alpha, but he ain't there yet. If Arthur T. graduates, though, *Bobbey Ray the one.* He feels like asking Arthur T. for a rest. That old bothersomeness is itching in him today. 'Bout to boil up inside. First, he was going to give that redheaded bitch a barbering. Now he can't cause Mr. Carpenter heard him. Bobbey Ray's blood, almost always at a simmer, is heating up. But he ain't going to mess with Arthur T. At football practice he just might bust somebody's head open, though.

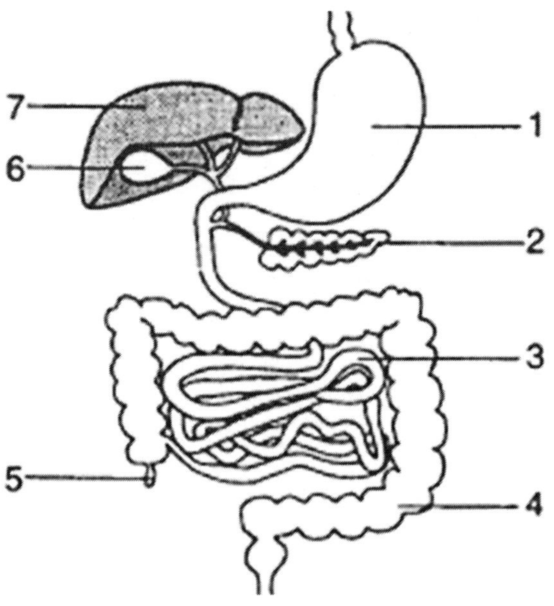

34. The diagram above represents the digestive system of a student who has eaten a healthy sandwich consisting of two slices of Sunbeam bread, a yummy slab of fried Spam, lettuce, and Duke's mayonnaise. The final reactions for the complete hydrolysis of the bread would occur in organ (a.) 1 (b.) 2 (c.) 3 (d.) 4 (e.) 5

35. Which organ produces a substance that would be used in the emulsification of the lipids in the mayonnaise? (a.) 1 (b.) 2 (c.) 3 (d.) 4 (e.) 7

36. In which organs would chemical digestion of the Spam take place? (a.) 1 and 3 (b.) 1 and 7 (c.) 2 and 6 (d.) 3 and 5

Sixty steps down the hall, Mary Ellen Cartwright has been unsuccessful in her attempts to contact Liz Welch. First, she had a hell of a time finding the misfiled index card that holds vital information on Sandy: blood type (O positive), name of physician (Howard Snyder), next of kin (Peggy Welch of Honeycutt, Connecticut), etc. Mrs. Palmer tried at first, but after twenty minutes turned the job over to Mary Ellen, who has been instructed to call every five minutes. Once connected, she is to tell Mrs. Welch not to be alarmed but that Mrs. Palmer would like to speak to her. Mrs. Palmer will inform Mrs. Welch of the note and suggest that she not let Sandy leave the house. Of course, having to interrupt whatever she's doing every five minutes to make a futile call prevents Mary Ellen from accomplishing anything substantial. She has decided to paint her fingernails, and the pungent odor of the polish wafts through the glass-enclosed offices.

***

Of the various "Beauty Parlors" in Summerville, Minnie Finucan enjoys the greatest prestige, especially among the smart set who belong to George Miler Country Club. Oh, if you're looking for a Pentecostal Mt. Sinai-do, Patty Ruth Chaplin's your gal, but if you're looking for a smart clipped frosted coif and don't mind paying extra, you'll get your hair done at 55 Richardson Avenue where Minnie is holding court along with fellow cosmetologists Emma Brown and Terri Sessions. Only two of the three chairs are in use. Liz Welch hasn't shown yet for her eleven o'clock, which is typical. It's going to, of course, throw everything off whack as far as scheduling goes.

Anne Jensen almost called to cancel her appointment today considering AJ's disappearance, but reconsidering, she thought it best to go about her business as if he were in school. Sitting by the phone is no way to spend such a beautiful day, and besides, Eva Mae, the housekeeper, is at home if AJ arrives before the end of school, which Anne considers extremely unlikely. She arrives promptly at eleven fifteen just as Cindy is finishing with Joanne Elder, who wears her hair shoulder length, as if she were a teenager or something. Emma Brown does Anne's hair, so ironically enough, it's Minnie Finucan, the most sought-after stylist, who finds herself unemployed now. It's a situation that makes her uncomfortable.

"Good morning, Anne," Minnie chirps in an overfriendly drawl. "What a gorgeous day!"

"It certainly is," Anne says, looking forward to the ensuing half-hour of small talk, gossip, and character assassination, especially since there's a *bone fide* mystery in this small uneventful town, the mystery of the death of that Trotter boy, and Anne would like to hear the latest town gossip on that score. It hasn't been that hot a topic among her circle of friends, the Reach Out Committee at St. Paul's, or her bridge club. However, because she has a rebellious teenager herself, she can't help wondering if illicit drugs played a role.

As Anne leans back to have Cindy wash her hair, she says, "Minnie, I don't know that I've ever been in here and seen you not cutting somebody's hair."

"Well, looks like I'm getting stood up," she says brusquely. "Seems like she could at least call."

"Maybe she's had a flat tire or something," Cindy says.

Given the tragic events of last week in which the Welches were main players, you might suspect that Minnie Finucan would be more tolerant of Liz's tardiness, but the fact of the matter is that Liz is *always* late for her appointments, slurring her apologies, and sure enough, almost as soon as "flat tire" is out of Cindy's mouth, enter Liz, bustling, mouthing *mea culpas*, hoping that she's not caused any inconvenience.

"Not at all," Minnie lies, deciding that she's going to make short work of Liz with a quick wash and superfast cut.

"Oh, my what a week," Liz says theatrically, as she reclines in Minnie's central chair. "I hope none of you will ever have to endure a week like this."

***

Jill Birdsong has come to school prepared. She is hypersensitive to the symptoms but also super thrifty. She wishes now, however, that she had gone ahead at activity period and taken care of what wasn't yet a problem, because now, suddenly, it feels like a problem. It couldn't happen at a more awkward time. "Excuse me, Rozier," she says, her eyes darting down to linoleum. Rozier, in another dimension, the hero of his on-going football fantasy, blinks. The cartoon bubble floating above his head pops and dissipates. Before he can respond, Jill's walking away from him, headed to Mrs. Middleton's desk. Teacher and student sidle away together to the corner next to the door. Rozier wonders if Jill's tattling on him for not helping during the experiment. She's whispering into Mrs. Middleton's ear. Rozier looks to his right where Ollie had just finished pouring some liquid or element or something into a container as Cindy hands him a cover. When he looks back up, Jill's gone. Not in the room.

Rozier looks down at the various implements and chemicals of the experiment. He leans over to the measuring vessel but doesn't smell a thing. Shit, he hasn't been paying attention. What if Jill's gone home sick? Shit, he's a step behind. He takes the cover off the container and pours in the liquid, sulfuric acid (H_2SO_4).

***

As Will approaches his driveway, he ejects the Hendrix tape and pops in Big Brother and the Holding Company—*four gentlemen and one great, great broad*—then brakes for the gravelly incline that rises between the two-foot, moss-grown brick walls that flank the front of his house. The shadows of the oak trees darken the interior of the bus, broken suddenly by stuttering sunlight. AJ has turned all his attention to Mr. Peabody, whose grateful eyes nevertheless project the sorrows of the centuries. Will is taking it slow and smiles to see that his mother's car is missing, but then, as he rounds the bend to the carriage house, he slams on the brakes, lurching dog, passenger, tapes, driver.

They both shout, "The red Mustang!"

"Jinx," they both say.

***

41. Which substance is a nutrient in the human diet?

(a.) oxygen (b.) carbon dioxide (c.) roughage (d.) water

42. After food enters the small intestine, lipases, proteases, and amylases are secreted into the small intestine by the:

a.) liver (b.) pancreas (c.) mouth (d.) large intestine

43. Why are human feces generally yellow in color?

(a.) carbohydrates (b.) oxidation (c.) a reddish-yellow bile pigment, $C_{33}H_{36}N_4O_6$, derived from the degradation of heme (d.) mastication

Steve Murray is a tall, very blonde, ruddy-faced boy with a somewhat queasy stomach. This test is sort of starting to get to him. Not because he's not doing well, but because it's almost like he can smell what's going on in the test. It's like he can smell the shit. It's getting worse. He looks up to see several students distracted. In the front of the room, Mrs. Laban is frowning, standing on her tiptoes, then lowering herself, standing on her tiptoes, lowering, sniffing like a birddog.

***

By the time Will and AJ have clambered up the porch steps, Rusty and Sandy are on their feet, smoothing out their clothes.

"Fancy meeting you here," AJ says as he steps over an old encyclopedia Will has left on the floor.

"Hey, Russ," Will says. "Hey, Sandy."

"Hello."

As soon as she sees Mr. Peabody, Sandy makes a beeline, talking baby dog talk.

"Hey, man," Will says. "I got some bad news."

Rusty's grinning. "Oh no, don't tell me that the school's burned down."

Will's not smiling. "Look man, the police are looking for you. Well, if not for you, for a red Mustang."

Rusty laughs.

"No, man. I'm not kidding. Dickey came up to AJ and me and asked us if we knew anybody with a red Mustang."

Rusty's still not taking the bait. "Hey, Sandy. You didn't rob a bank before you picked me up, did you? Will says the cops are after a red Mustang."

Sandy looks up, confused, leans her head back and shakes her hair.

"He's serious, man," AJ says.

The smile on Rusty's face fades. "You're jiving me."

"Look, man, I'm holding," Will says. "I can't have the police coming 'round here."

Rusty still seems incredulous. "You're serious?"

"Goddamn it, Rusty. We're not kidding."

Rusty turns to Sandy, who seems strangely unconcerned. "Sandy, do you have any idea why the police are looking for you?"

Sandy looks up from her squatting position next to Mr. Peabody. "Police. Why would the police be looking for me?"

"Maybe, it's a different red Mustang they're looking for," Rusty says.

AJ sounds exasperated, "A red Mustang is a red Mustang is a red Mustang."

"Well, if we haven't done anything wrong, we don't have anything to worry about. Right, Sandy?" Rusty asks looking down at her still squatting next to Mr. Peabody.

As she starts to stand, Sandy stumbles slightly.

"Excuse me," she says. "I sort of feel sick."

And before she can get to the kitchen sink or bathroom, she vomits – not on the rug but on the warped pine floors of the hall leading to the bathroom.

***

Jill's in a hurry to get back to class, so she's washing her hands quickly under running water. The only hand drying option is one of those revolving cloth towel contraptions where God knows who or what has dried her/its hands. Before Jill can reach for the paper towels in her purse, she hears the startling, pulsating horn buzz of the fire alarm. They usually warn you in advance when they're having a drill. She hurriedly pushes open the restroom door to see students already walking single file toward the exits. Not sure what to do, she walks abreast one of the lines, and now she smells it. Not something burning but something awful. Maybe it is something burning. Something like rubber. Something chemical.

***

Liz Welch's tales of woe have had the salutary effect of erasing AJ's disappearance from Anne Jensen's mind. Liz has breached some borders, for example, providing details that Anne certainly wouldn't have shared: for example, the

166

physical singularities of Tripp's pre-embalmed body. Fortunately, laid out in their chairs, the ladies can't turn and make eye contact with one another, their lines of vision being dictated by the beauticians who manually turn their clients' heads as they continue to snip and pick.

***

Across campus, Bobbey Ray hears the fire alarm beneath construction sounds. He screeches a shrill whistle, and as the racket subsides, they all listen to the distant aooga.

"Looks like a fire drill," Arthur T. says.

"Reckon they don't care if we get burn up in a fire," Bucky Gaskins says, scratching his armpit.

"Why you say that," Arthur T. asks.

"Ain't no alarms go off here to warn us."

"We outside, bo. How they gone to set up an alarm outside? Hang one on a cloud?"

Bucky points across campus. "Look at 'em."

"Them hippies."

"Come on, bo. Some on them ain't so bad."

"Like who?"

"Mike Moore. I'd drink a PBR with Mike Moore any day," Arthur T. says.

"That's different. He's on the team," Bucky says.

"He's still a hippie," Arthur T. counters. "Wears them flower belts. Growing his hair as long as Coach will let him."

"I still say it's different," Bucky insists.

167

Bobbey Ray has his hand extended above his eyebrows, shielding his eyes. "One of these days I'm gone to give one of them bitches a barbering. First thing I'm gonna do after we win State."

"Now you talkin', Bobbey," Bucky says.

***

Ollie is agonizing as he walks out in single file, following Mrs. Middleton to their designated spot on the northeast corner of the waterless reflecting pond in the Junior Courtyard. What if Jill, wherever she was—he suspects, "indisposed"—had been overcome by the fumes and passed out? In the movies, the hero breaks away and dashes back into the flaming building (make that the hydrogen-sulfide-suffused building) to lift the unconscious damsel in his arms and carry her to safety. But the heroes in movies are not necessarily rational. Chances are that Jill heard—how couldn't she—the earsplitting alarm and reached safety by an alternative route. The judicious thing would be to ask Mrs. Middleton about Jill's absence rather than dashing off to an undisclosed location like a maniac. So, Ollie approaches a panic-stricken Mindy Middleton who is thumbing through her gradebook.

"Mrs. Middleton," Ollie says, "the only student missing is Jill Birdsong. I've counted."

"Oh my God, Ollie!"

"It's probably okay. Where was she heading?"

Mrs. Middleton is tall and thin, a sort of female scarecrow. "I pray that she got out all right."

"I bet she did," Ollie says. "That alarm is ear-piercing."

168

Rusty has younger brothers and sisters. He's changed diapers and cleaned up vomit. Only, without asking permission, he throws away the towels he has used to clean up the mess in the garbage can outside. He'll lift a couple from his house to replace them. He's in a hurry to see how Sandy's doing, passing from bright sunlight to the dark and dingy carriage house. Sandy is on the corduroy green couch mortified.

"Sandy, how you feeling?"

"I'm so embarrassed."

Will says, "It's okay. I assure you, you're not the first one to vomit on these floors. Missing the rug is a bonus."

"Yes, this is a den of iniquity, all right," Rusty adds.

"Remember that time Janie Jones got into that Boone's Farm?" Will asks, holding Mr. Peabody by the collar.

AJ's feigning illness, holding his stomach, staggering. "Shut up, man. You gonna have me puking if you retell that one."

Rusty heads toward the kitchen. "Sandy, let me get you a drink of water."

Rusty knows where the glasses are kept, but there are none in the kitchen cabinet, only two jelly jars and a coffee cup. He decides on a jar because the coffee cup is a hand-me-down, dainty, chipped blue and white Wedgwood Willow imitation that would hardly hold enough H_2O to get your whistle wet.

The jar's podunk-looking, so he opens the fridge in search of ice, thinking a couple of cubes might add some dignity. The ice trays are plastic, worse for the wear, and who ever refilled them last time did a lousy job, the ice uneven and shallow. Rusty scoots over the sink and twists the trays, and the cubettes pop forth raining like hail into the discolored porcelain sink. He yanks the last paper towel from the roll lying on its side on the counter and wraps it around the jar.

As he carries it to Sandy in the den, far off sirens sound.

***

"That's a fire truck," Minnie says, an expert in identifying sirens.

The Fire Department isn't far from Richardson, on East North Main just across the train tracks from Mrs. Fortunak's Boarding House.

Anne Jensen has suddenly turned white. "Damn it, Alex," she thinks.

"Yep, that's a fire truck," Minnie says. I don't hear any ambulances or police cars yet, but they're bound to be joining in directly.

"Itn't it funny," Cindy Sessions says, "how whenever you hear a siren, you automatically think it's somebody you love, and it never is."

Liz Welch says hoarsely, "I'd knock on wood if I were you."

"No," Anne Jensen says, "never say never."

***

Dickey gets the call as he's pulling up to Bacon's Bridge and immediately turns around and flips the switch for the siren. Back at school, Principal Pushcart has assembled his Emergency Action team. Wisely, he keeps his laminated emergency procedures sheet in the right-hand desk drawer and therefore has it in his hand. He's dispatched Vice Principal Dodds to the Junior Courtyard outside of the science wing to find Mrs. Middleton, figuring that a chemistry experiment has gone haywire or something. Damn, he's not smelled anything so awful since he was in the army and had latrine patrol.

When Mr. Dodds finds Mrs. Middleton, she's on the verge of panic. Her own marital dissatisfactions, which had seemed so important a half hour an ago, have diminished to the point of dissipation.

"John, John, I'm missing a student," she says. Mr. Dodds is a young-looking sixty, slender, nattily dressed in khakis and a blue blazer. He parts his fine, blondish-white hair in the middle.

Calm, cool as a cucumber. "Who?"

"Jill Birdsong."

While the rest of the class is raucously discussing, if not celebrating, the unfortunate turn of events, Ollie is hovering next to Mrs. Middleton and Mr. Dodds. Because Mrs. Middleton seems incapable of uttering any information, Ollie chimes in, "She left the classroom before the alarm. I think she was maybe going to the restroom."

Mr. Dodds asks, "Is this correct, Mindy?"

She sort of sobs, swallows, nods her head.

Ollie has taken over. "If she had heard the alarm in the girls' restroom, she possibly might have exited down the opposite end of the hallway and be across the building on the other side."

"Very good," Mr. Dodds says. "Your name's Wyborn, isn't it?"

"Yes, sir."

"Mr. Wyborn, why don't you head over there and see if you can find her."

Ollie vigorously nods his head. "Yes, sir!"

***

Down the road a piece, Will has summoned Rusty outside to find out the scoop, and he has recounted the adventures of the morning: AJ's departure, the cross-examination in Pushcart's office, Sandy's picking him up thumbing, the haircut. Rusty doesn't, though, share with Will his sexual change in status, from virgin to guilt-racked potential sire.

The sirens have multiplied manyfold, and Rusty hasn't heard anything quite like this since Mr. Moore crashed his twin-engine plane in the woods next to the airport.

"I wonder what's going on?" he says to Will.

"Something bad," Will says.

The sirens are getting louder and louder as the town's two fire trucks and two ambulances streak past, horns blowing, diminishing as they speed their way toward school.

"So, you want Sandy and me to split, I take it."

"I hate to man, but like I said, I'm holding."

"Where's it hidden?"

"Out back in the shed in an old toolbox."

"And you actually think with all this commotion, the cops are gonna intuit that the red Mustang is hidden in the

172

back of your yard and draw up a warrant to search your house for drugs just in case the Mustang's there and just in case there might be some pot on the premises?"

"Man, I love you," Will says.

"Huh."

"You're right. Forget it. I was a tad bit paranoid. Look, AJ and I are in the process of launching the USS Kerouac. We were gonna contact you after school."

"What?"

"Yeah, man. And with this commotion, it'll be a lot easier. Send Sandy on her merry way. I'm in the process of getting a trailer hitch put on the bus, and we're gonna launch it at Eddie's country house."

"I can't send Sandy on her merry way."

"Why not?"

"She's been eating some sort of pills. She's in no condition to drive."

"You don't reckon she's vomited them up?"

"I hadn't thought of that. Maybe. Maybe not."

"I'll tell you what. You stay here with her and Mr. Peabody, AJ and I will head downtown to take care of the hitch. We'll come back to pick you up when we're done, and you can figure out what you're gonna do with Sandy."

"Okay," Rusty says, relieved, liking the idea of buying some time.

***

Ollie has been blessed with the ability to conceptualize spatial reality and so has determined the most likely exit Jill would have taken if indeed she had headed the opposite way up the hall as he has theorized. Of course, there's no guarantee that she would have stayed put. Indeed, it's likely that she might try to find her chemistry classmates, so as Ollie makes his way around the building, he's keeping a sharp lookout for Jill, turning his head to the right and left, using his peripheral vision, slowing somewhat when he sees groups where she might socialize.

He walks right past Camilla Creel without noticing her standing several steps away from her nearest classmate. Ollie strides right past Althea and James, who are smiling and nodding their heads. He doesn't spot Davis Bolster and Josh Silverstein as they attempt to slap each other's hands.

As he rounds the corner, a flicker of motion catches his eyes. Most of the students are in clumps around their teachers, so it's a fairly static configuration. Ollie skirts to his right, to pass Mrs. Pinsky's history class to see if he can see who it is walking—a girl—oh yes, Jill! No doubt trying to find her class. He calls out, "Jill, Jill Birdsong…" and she stops, cocking her ear. "Jill, it's me Ollie. I've been sent by Mr. Dodds to see if I could find you. We've been worried about you."

Jill stops and smiles at seeing a friendly face, but then frowns at the realization that she's the cause of anxiety.

Ollie is smiling from ear to ear. Everything's okay. He reaches for her hand, grabs it. "Come on," he says exultantly. "I'll lead you back to the class."

"What in the world's going on?" she asks, continuing to hold his hand as they walk back toward the corner of the building.

"I don't know exactly," Ollie says, "I suspect that somebody in lab wasn't paying attention and screwed the experiment up, letting out a dangerous cloud of hydrogen sulfide. If not sealed in a closed container, it certainly would clear the building."

"Is it dangerous?" Jill asks.

"Maybe," Ollie says. "It's quite poisonous, but I don't think it's explosive or anything. It sure does stink, though."

"That's the understatement of the year," Jill says, letting go of his hand.

Book 2: Beneath Surfaces

"Somebody spoke, and I went into a dream."

John Lennon

Early Afternoon

Tripp
Plop
Splash.

After he found Dana's note. Spying. Going through the purse.

Blue veins bulging around the corner from his eye. Blue vein, blue eye.

Did you let him kiss you? Tell me!

Tripp!

Tell me!

Yes.

Tripp

Plop

Splash.

You let him feel your tittie?

Tripp, where you going? Come back. Tripp.

Please, God, let my period come.

What was that? Pebble patter on the window. His face like a moon outside. Like a little boy. Heartbroken. Tears streaming down his face. Looking so much younger with those squinty red raw cried out eyes. His bottom lip, trembling.

Oh-oh-pen the wind-oh, bitch.

Shhhhhhhhhhhhhhhhhh, Tripp.

Never again. You'll never see me again.

Don't talk like that. Go home. Don't overreact. No, it's not our last kiss.

A kiss through the screen. Tiny little mesh between.

Terrified tires screeching scream, lights coming on.

Tripp

Plop.

Splat.

Rusty says to Sandy, "They're gone."

"I know. You just told me. They've gone to get a trailer hitch."

"No, the sirens."

"The sirens?"

"They're gone. I don't hear the sirens."

"No, I don't hear them either."

"I wonder what it is. Or was. No, is. Some disaster."

Rap-rap-stallion. You're a rap-rap-stallion. Sweet and funny. Red down there, too. Littler. Little freckled scared hands. Will's the pick of the litter, though.

Sandy, snapping out of her reverie, "I bet those guys hate me."

"What guys?"

"Will and AJ."

"Why do you say that?"

"Well, like, I vomited on the floor."

Rusty, smiling, "If those guys hated everyone that vomited on these floors, they wouldn't have any friends. I could conjure up for you a quick epic catalogue of pukers, human and feline. Let's see:

As when Etna shoots forth froths of fire,
so vomited Glenn Felix, lava like,
onto Weeza's Persian rug.

Oh, no, Mrs. Laban's test.
(But it's too late, baby blue,
Cause it's all over now).

No use to cry over spilt milk,
Spilt semen.
Science books.
The French I took.

Rusty, doing his patented Foghorn Leghorn imitation, "I say, vomiting on this floor don't amount to even a misdemeanor."

Sandy feigns a Southern accent, "Hey, bo, I love the way you talk."

"Hey, I love the way you smile."

Jesus, did I actually say that? A B-movie embarrassing cliché. What if Will overheard me say that? Should I kiss her?

"Hey, Sandy, can I get all pedantic on you and play you a song on the stereo? Do you know the song, 'A Day in the Life?' The Beatles?"

"I dunno. It doesn't sound familiar."

Rusty grabs a pillow from the other end of the sofa. "Just lean back there and be comfortable. You're in for a treat. Need more water? You feel okay?"

"I'm fine."

"This is a bad habit of mine," Rusty says. "I force people to listen to music I like and lecture them on it. But it's worth it for the not un-hip listener. Because the music is magical. Worthwhile. Like, a brief chronicle of the times. Hey, but no jive, this "Day in the Life" song is a revelation. Listen to like a child, with an open mind."

Suffer the children.

"Well, go ahead, I'm all ears," Sandy says.

"Good, 'cause it's a song you gotta listen to. The words, I mean. It's like a short story mixed with a movie, mixed with a symphony."

"Well, play it all right already!"

"You sure?"

"Do I have a choice?"

Oh, God I need a cigarette.

"Is there an ashtray around here?"

Rusty leans over the turntable. "It's against the rules to smoke in here. Will would go apeshit. His ol' man died of lung cancer."

"Oh. Really?"

"Yes. He's a puritan when it comes to that. Makes John Calvin looks like Hugh Hefner. But, shhhhhhhhhhhhhhhhhh, listen."

(Crackle)

Heard the news today, oh boy […] and though the news was sad […] just had to laugh […] out in a car […] didn't notice […] a crowd of people […] oh, boy […] people turned […] I'd…love…to…turn …you […] Woke up […] dragged a comb across my head […] in seconds flat […] the holes […] they had to count them […] now they know […] I'd…love…to…turn…you…on.

"What do you think?" Rusty asks as the stylus returns and the turntable clicks off.

"It's weird!"

"Sort of symphonic."

"Could I smoke a cig outside?" she asks.

Rusty sighs. "Sure, just don't throw the butt in the yard."

Outside, the day has ripened, the breeze picking up, the leaves shimmering. Rusty skips down the steps, Sandy in his wake, the shadows of the trees morphing in puddles on the ground. Rusty watches as Sandy walks her surprisingly stiff little walk to the Mustang to retrieve her cigs. Her legs are too skinny for her big-bosomed torso, but Rusty suddenly loves that disproportion about her. He loves everything about her. She sort of liked the song, maybe. He watched her face. Not everyone can share his enthusiasms. *Zombie nation.* Vickie, his short-lived girlfriend, into blandness, the Guess Who, for Christ sake. He's headed to the shed to borrow a pinch of Will's stash.

In the toolbox somewhere.

Dark and musty. Jars of screws. The USS Kerouac. Looks almost fake. Disneyesque. They want to head out tomorrow. *No can do.* Cans of congealed house paint. *Mold and mildew.* Spider webs. The ghosts of Civil War infantrymen. Cigar boxes of vacuum tubes. *Where's that toolbox? In the corner?*

Her voice outside, alarmed: Rusty, oh no, Rusty!

He runs from shed shadow to bright sunshine.

Sandy shouts, "He's gone!"

"Who?"

"The puppy dog. Mr. Peabody!"

Oh shit.

"Maybe he's in the house," Rusty says.

Shit!

Rusty pokes his head in the door. "Here puppy, puppy. Mr. Peeeeeeeeee Boddddddddddd Deeeeeeeeeeeee! Mr. Peeeeeeeeee Boddddddddddd Deeeeeeeeeeeee!"

The bane of my existence: carelessness. Dog, gone. Granddaddy Blanton: Dog gone it. I sing of the wrath of Will.

"Mr. Peeeeeeeeee Boddddddddddd Deeeeeeeeeeeee!"

Rusty runs to the front yard, where the heavy traffic might be, *no dead dog, please*, acorns and fallen pinecones crunching under his high-top Converse Allstars. Not a sign of life. But here comes a Ford Falcon station wagon, with kids, hanging out the window, yodeling, hollering, screeching rebel yells, fishtailing on purpose. Joey Brown, David Kaczor, the twins Debby and Robyn Kellam. *What time is it? What period? 5A – lunch? The test gone. What different worlds.* He imagines himself in the class instead of playing a postlapsarian record. *Mrs. Laban, like a statue, standing with her feet crossed in front of her, a charm school mannerism, learned, orchestrated, fake,* Mr. Peeeeeeeeee Boddddddddddd Deeeeeeeeeeeee!

Sandy's in the backyard, statuary, cats, calico, weeds, a slight terrace, *no.* Mr. Peeeeeeeeee Boddddddddddd Deeeeeeeeeeeee!

***

Hambone has dodged a Dodge Dart as he scampers across Highway 17-A, the scent of Daisy long gone, the vehicle a reflecting alien rush of war cry. The horn dopplering.

Mr. Peeeeeeeeee Boddddddddd Deeeeeeeeeeee!

***

Football practice ain't been called off. Four o'clock sharp. Ain't every day you get off school early, you know. Bobbey Ray Bosheen watches Arthur T. Hall's jacked-up Pontiac GTO with 4-on-the-floor, a 455 cubic inch V8, Hooker headers, dual exhaust. It's laying down 'bout a quarter inch of Goodyear rubber, smoking as he shakes his tail out of the parking lot. *Arthur T don't give a shit.* Back at the school, flashing PO-lice and fire truck lights going all psycheeeeedelic.

Bobbey Ray takes the morning. school bus from Stallsville, but even though he ain't on the team, Bucky Gaskins gives him and the boys a ride to practice in the back of his old beat-up but big-engine Ford pickup truck. Them that's riding the bus have to stay in the Cafetorium in a study hall 'til 3 p.m., but Bobbey Ray's one of the lucky ones, headed to the poolhall. Arthur T. even luckier. He's headed to Sweat's to pick up a 6-pack of PBR and drink it behind Cooder Knight's barn. Son of a bitch! If Bobbey Ray was Bucky, he sure as hell would be going with Arthur T, but that ain't gonna work cause Arthur T can't stand that little sawed-off sumbitch. Hell yeah. School's out. A miracle. Ol' man Pushcart making announcements out of that electrificated cheerleader thingamajig. Bobbey Ray lets go his bloodcurdling rebel yell, passed down from Bosheen to Bosheen since the Battle of Grimball's Landing. That sets off a chain reaction of rebel yells.

A football field away, pacing back and forth across the quadrangle, Dr. Horton shakes his head and mumbles "Visigoths."

***

Ollie, too, takes the bus to and from school, so the underclassman parking lot is an exotic locale for him. Some of those non-college-prep boys are bellowing strange animal calls or something over at the senior lot, but Ollie's not aware of many animals that sound quite like that; then again, he's not what you would call an outdoorsman. Jill and Kathi and Nanci and Patti usually ride together in Jill's '67 Camaro, but today Jill has offered Ollie a ride home, and Patti's catching a lift with Billy, her date for the homecoming dance. So, it's just Ollie and the three girls. The way people are carrying on, you'd think the war had ended or something. Ollie recalls a photo he's seen of a sailor kissing a nurse at the end of the Second World War. It could be Colonel Dukenfield for all he knows, but no, it was a sailor not an Air Force pilot.

***

The Colonel, in fact, is as happy as the kids. Because of his gout, he has been excused from accounting for the students, marshalling them toward the Cafetorium or out to the parking lots. Habitually, he pats the pocket of his frayed tweed jacket to feel the comforting bulk of his flask. The rumor is some chemistry experiment gone wrong. He'd like to reward the palooka who screwed up with a crisp dollar

183

bill. As celebratory students caper past, he bellows a hearty, "Yahoo to you, too, young men."

"Aooga," he adds, pulling an invisible rope as he sees scowling Eula Lynne Laban across the square with gradebook in hand, ushering some orange-headed lass toward the Cafetorium. To look at Eula Lynne, you'd think that she'd just lost fifty good men to the Jerrys. *The Republic will survive methinks.*

"Excuse me," he calls out to Quinn Burke, who also brandishes a gradebook. "Young Mr. Burke."

Quinn, who's standing around looking official, says, "Yes, sir, Colonel."

Kids are flowing past, smiling.

"And, Mr. Burke, may I ask what your official function is at this particular post?"

"Hell, I don't know," says Quinn. "I'm just trying to look like I know what I'm doing."

"I have a better idea, lad. When's the last time you've visited the local chapter of the Veteran of Foreign Wars hut?"

"Not being a veteran, 4F to boot, never."

"Then perhaps you'd like to abscond from our present location and accompany me to the cozy confines of the VA Hut. I promise you; no one around here will be the wiser, and the Hut is a veritable living museum, a storehouse of firsthand recollection. Whiskey, beer, Pearl Harbor, Guadalcanal, D-Day. The drinks are on me, lad. It'll help you when you're teaching history to those kids. Much more productive than hanging around here."

"Colonel, I'm a math teacher. I'm in your department. Remember?"

"Details, my son. Merely details."

"Hell, why not," Quinn grins, and offers his arm to the Colonel.

***

James Hooper drives a black Studebaker that his great Aunt Lou (his paternal grandfather's sister) gave him for his sixteenth birthday, an exquisitely maintained oddity with checkered upholstery and a front grill that makes it look like one of those talking cars from the 1930s cartoons, *Gandy Goose. Honk honk. Home again, home again, jiggedy-jig.* In his upstairs room awaits his own little world and the model he's been constructing of his dream house. Drawings, blueprints, balsawood, glue. He works hours and hours in his spare time. Meg and Althea have invited him over to Meg's to check out some records, but, no, he'd rather go home and work on the project listening to his own music, his Smetana and Borodin, not their Joni Mitchell and James Taylor.

He has parked the Studebaker far away from the other cars, and already tons of people have left, the students being excused in segments. Seniors first, then juniors…the poor pre-drivers, freshmen and the like, have been relegated to the Cafetorium, a monstrosity of space that might make a prison mess hall look cheerful. Every time he approaches his car, he feels a slight prick of dread, the worry that "faggot" might appear in soap, or worse, but as James makes a quick reconnaissance, he smiles. Key in the door. The old musty smell of Aunt Lou's life – somehow even her perfume still lingers postmortem. The heavy door slams.

***

Eula Lynne is beside herself. This is a real disaster. The tests she worked so hard to compose are utterly ruined. No longer viable. She'll have to start from scratch, change the questions, but that's going to skew the topics she wants to stress. Coming up with two tests overnight is going to be a Herculean labor. Why did the test have to be today? That durn Middleton woman not supervising those glandular fools the way she should have. Eula Lynne sees Kevin Manigault headed the wrong way to the parking lot when he should be headed for study hall.

"Excuse me, Kevin," she says. "Where do you think you're going? You're supposed to be in the Cafetorium with the rest of the bus riders."

"But, Ma'am," he says, "I don't ride the bus."

"You don't? You live 'round here?"

"No, Ma'am. I live in Germantown."

"You do?"

"Yes, Ma'am. I drive myself to school. I got my own car."

"You do?"

"Yes, Ma'am."

"Oh, okay, run along then."

***

Back at the poolhall, Eddie is explaining to Will and AJ that no matter how cool a trailer hitch they are affixing to that VW bus, there's no way that weak thing with its eggbeater engine's going to have the horsepower to haul a raft whose bottom is composed of twenty-four six-inch diameter pine logs. He suggests they follow him home in the big truck.

Just then the door opens and in walks Bobbey Ray, Bucky, Eddie Droze, and Lonnie Bishop like some outlaws from a Spaghetti Western, hombres up to no goddamn good.

"Uh oh," AJ says, "as our friend Rusty would say, 'the better part of valor.'"

"What does that mean?" Eddie asks.

"I'm not quite sure," AJ says, "but whenever he says it, the gist is, 'let's get the hell out of Dodge.'"

"Yep," Will says, "Rusty might be a wuss, but he's a smart wuss. I say let's get the hell out of Dodge and continue this conversation outside."

So as Bobbey Ray and his crew lumber their way to the bar, Eddie, AJ, and Will cut behind tables 1 and 2 and step outside into the shadow of the awning that runs along the front of the otherwise sun-splashed sidewalk. A golden Camaro, no doubt looking for a parking space, creeps past, then disappears around the same corner.

Buzz, too, has noted Bobbey Ray's entrance. He's pretty sure he's told that Bosheen boy he never wanted to see his ass in here again, but shorthanded and facing a glut of unexpected customers, Buzz decides to play it by ear. It's when he's drunk that Bobbey Ray's a problem, and if he's just come home from school, chances are he's all right.

Doesn't make sense to make a scene. He won't sell him any alcohol, though.

***

As Jill rounds the corner, Kathi suggests that they circle the block to see if a space opens up. They've decided to have delicious poolhall hotdogs, and Ollie, of course, is going inside to place the order.

"If there's not a space this go around," Ollie suggests, "you can drop me off, and I'll run in and place the order."

Just then a pick-up truck flies by with two boys standing up in the bed. "Wow, that's stupid," Nanci says.

"Natural selection at work," Ollie says. "Hey, something really weird happened to me at school today."

"Oh yeah?"

"Yeah, I went to the gym to get a pop and this girl can't operate the machine, and I help her, and you know what she says?"

The girls giggle.

"What?"

"You call Cokes pop," Kathi says. "But go on. What happened?"

"Anyway," Ollie continues, "I help her get a carbonated drink, and she says, 'Thank you, sir,' like I'm some kind of adult or something."

"How old was she, the girl that called you sir?" Nanci asks.

"I'm not sure. In high school. I've seen her around. She has orange sort of curly, sort of frizzy, hair."

"Oh my god, Fang!"

"Kathi, that's not nice," Jill says.

"C'mon, Jill… If I said her name, whatever it is, half of y'all wouldn't know who I was talking about."

"Yeah, "Jill says, "you got a point."

Jill slows and pulls to a stop. "Okay, I'm going to jump out right here," Ollie says. "Find a place or keep circling the block. I'll be back ASAP."

***

On the sidewalk outside the poolhall, Eddie and the boys are coordinating their plan to haul the raft to Limehouse Landing.

"Oh my God," AJ says. "Here comes Ollie Wyborn!"

"Who's he?" Will asks.

"A kid in my homeroom. If he's headed for the poolhall, it could mean only one of two things."

"What's that?"

"It's either a sign of the Apocalypse, or that accident at school let off some mind-altering air-borne substance."

"Hey, Ollie," AJ calls out as Ollie steps up on the curb, "Man, what in the hell's going on?"

Ollie, whose mind is awash in rapid serotonin chain reactions, hasn't noticed that AJ is among the trio of boys standing in the shadows of the awning, and AJ's presence spooks him. After all, he's just plagiarized AJ's natural selection line, and – poof – suddenly he appears out of nowhere, as if in a dream, his conscience made flesh, a voice from the shadows of Freudian theory no less. Ollie shivers as an adrenaline rush sweeps up his spinal cord.

AJ repeats, "Ollie."

"Oh, hello, AJ. Sorry. I'm just surprised to run into you."

AJ uses his WC Fields voice. "Likewise, I'm sure," but then returns to his regular voice. "But, Ollie, man, hey, really. What the hell happened at school?"

"Oh man, someone goofed in chemistry class and created a toxic cloud of sulfuric hydroxide. I was there. That's definitely where it came from."

"You know who it was? Who it was that screwed up?" AJ asks.

Frowning, Ollie almost says, *yes, Rozier Ravenel*, but thinks better of it. "I can't say for sure. I'd love to chat, AJ, but I have to order some hotdogs-to-go."

"Just one more thing, Ollie, be very circumspect in there."

It surprises Ollie that AJ would use a word like circumspect. "Huh?"

"Be careful. Don't use words like 'chat' for example. It could get you hurt."

"I don't quite understand," Ollie says.

Eddie says impatiently, "Man, what he's saying is that they're seriously in-bred hillbillies in there that would just as soon cut a Yankee's ass as jack off. Keep a low profile. Walk softly."

"Thanks, I guess," Ollie says.

"See you."

Like his parents, Ollie is a Doubting Thomas. Fire and brimstone to him are natural phenomena, not the elements of an infernal furnace. Yet when Ollie steps into the smoky gloom of the pool hall, he finds himself thinking of illustrations he's seen of Hell. Not only that but it also smells weird in here. Sour and sweet. Body odor mixed with frying ground beef and stale beer and cigarette smoke. Some of these people look damaged. He understands why girls don't come in here. Too-loud, raucous voices and those strange vowel-rich inflections. *Whatyousaybo*, a greeting sounding more like Swahili than English. An older man with sergeant stripes on his uniform talks to and rocks a pinball machine with blinking lights and plastered with curvaceous cartoon women. Lights blink on and off and ding ding ding ding ding. The metal ball rolls up the incline but now down again. Flippers flip. Up the incline and down again. Beneath the ding, ding ding ding ding, the din of clacking pool balls, laughter, blended conversations. Recorded music from a jukebox, a familiar song spelling out a girl's name: G-L-O-R-I-A.

A line of about fifteen red swivel stools beneath a bar/lunch counter. Upon every stool sits a male: here an old, grizzled character with a white cane and a seeing eye German shepherd. The Old Blind Man Ollie's seen a couple of times at football games. Next to him, a paint-splattered, middle-aged man with a cigarette dangling from his mouth moving up and down as he talks. Others, all strangers, push their way between the stools to order. Ollie might as well be in Mozambique as far as knowing exactly the etiquette involved with ordering. There doesn't seem to be a pattern. Only two people taking and cooking orders for twenty. *Dog eat dog. Survival of the fittest.* Four guys wearing SHS shop overalls are sitting in a line, so he decides to lean between two of them to place his order.

Who this is here sticking his head here? Gotdamn round ol' timey hippie glasses.

"Excuse me, excuse me."

Ain't his turn sumbitch. Buzz better quit looking at me like that.
Go cut me a switch, Bobbey Ray, I teach you not to pay no attention to me. I thought I tole you to pick that room up.
Gotdamn round ol' timey hippie glasses.

Ollie tries to make eye contact with Buzz. *Why the dimness?* Behind the bar a tin sign in fading red all caps: NO PROFANITY. Carved coconut head monkey faces staring out from shelves behind the bar. Jars of rubberized eggs crowded in a murky solution. A print of dogs playing poker.

"Well, x-cuse you."

"Sorry. It's sort of crowded in here."

"Kiss my ass."

Circumspection. Circum = around; spec = to look, as in spectacles.

Looking around, then down the bar, Ollie spots a perhaps more congenial place to order and walks to the far end, farther away from the door. On the wall beyond the bar, he sees cue sticks lined on a rack with tiny padlocks.

Maybe he could dance to this song. G-L-O-R-I-I-I-I-IA!

J-I-Double L B-I-R-D-S-O-N-G

Jukebox: *Knock on my door*

***

At the Big House, no sign of Rusty, Sandy, or Mr. Peabody. "Damn," says AJ in a Boris Badanoff Russian accent. "Redhead Moose must have kidnapped dog."

"Mannish-Boykin, you mean?" Will asks. "I can't believe it. The cops are looking for that red Mustang, so what do they do? They drive off somewhere with my dog."

"Whatcha mean your dog? I'm the one who found him. Plus, he belongs to somebody else."

"Boys, boys," Eddie chides. "We can solve this custody battle later. I want to scope out this raft. Man, I can't believe you didn't let me in on this."

Past the meridian, the westward sun's shadows have softened the day into something like midafternoon. Yet the shed's dark, funky, the odor of old. Uncle Jerry's silly circa-1950s Citadel hat mildews on a shelf stacked with yellowed periodicals and a couple of old Citadel yearbooks, like artifacts in a dilapidated museum.

"Man, oh man," Eddie says, "I can't believe you built this thing."

"Well, we had a little help," AJ admits.

"From who? Admiral Rickover?"

"Well, not quite. John D. John."

Eddie laughs. "That freaking pervert! Did you have to let him suck you off?"

"Har har."

Eddie walks along the raft inspecting. "How y'all gonna steer this thing?"

"It's got a keel and some paddles, a couple of poles," Will says.

"You know what I'd add," Eddie says.

"What?" AJ asks.

"A little outboard motor."

"That'd be cheating," AJ says.

"Cheating who?" Eddie asks, turning to look at AJ. "You wouldn't have to use it, but if you got into trouble, it might come in handy. I got a little 6 horsepower Sears outboard I can lend you."

"I dunno," AJ says.

"Sure, cousin," Will says. "That sounds like a good idea. 'Judicious,' as Rusty would say."

"Well, help me back the truck up here and see if we can move this bad boy onto the trailer," Eddie says, the one in charge now.

***

As Jill rolls past the front of the pool hall yet again, Nanci says, "I wonder what could be keeping him so long? Daddy runs into the poolhall sometimes to pick up hotdogs, and it never takes this long."

"Maybe it's crowded with school out and everything," Kathi says.

"Well," Jill adds, "It seems unlikely to me that he'd run off with the money."

The girls laugh.

"That boy's sweet on you, Jill," Nanci says.

"You reckon?" Kathi says sarcastically as if it were way past obvious.

Jill blushes a deep crimson as she flips on her right turn signal.

"Well, I wish he'd hurry up," Nanci says. "My stomach doing its patented Elsa the Lion imitation."

***

Hambone follows the clicking in his brain as he enters the outskirts of the subdivision the Macys call home. It's way past his naptime. He's thirsty. He ignores the chattering squirrels above as his short, deformed-looking legs push onward. An ear pricks up.

Hambooooonnnnnnnnneeeeeeeeee!

A slight uptick of pace.

Hambooooonnnnnnnnneeeeeeeeee!

Hambone: Errrrrwooooooo!

Hambooooonnnnnnnnneeeeeeeeee!

And there he is trotting up to the edge of his half-acre yard. Little Eddie Macy sees Ham first and jumps up and down screaming in delight. His mother Joan turns and sees him, too. They rush to embrace him, throw their arms around him.

"You bad puppy," Joan says lovingly. "You bad, bad puppy. Up to no good I suspect."

Tail ticking, Hambone drools Colonel-like.

***

"Bobbey Ray, you see that sumbitch down at the end of the bar?" Bucky asks.

"You mean that queer-looking turd with them little ol' round granny glasses?"

"That's the one I'm talking about."

"Wanna cut his ass?"

"Not in broad daylight, bo. I got a better idea. When I was coming back from taking my leak, I seen him order seven hot dogs. I figured we might wait outside for him and take 'em off his hands, har har, if you know what I mean?"

"Now, bo that's a damn good idea. Go tell Lonnie and Eddie. I could stand to eat me another hot dog."

"Har har."

***

When John Bigelow gets back to the station, he flings his hat at the rack in the corner, a running joke, homage to Ian Fleming, and lo and behold, the hat catches the rack and teeters on the hook, and stays, the rack's rocking diminishing, the hat holding.

"Well, I'll be damned," Inez says. "Will miracles ever cease?"

John's ruined face breaks into a wincing smile, as if grinning is painful.

"You ever get that Welch woman?" he asks.

Inez looks straight up at the ceiling, exhaling deeply like they used to do in the noir movies, the smoke rising to the ceiling in a conical stream. "Yes, sir, and she sounded as drunk as a skunk."

He remembers pulling Liz Welch over a while back. *Now you get on home. I'm going to follow you. Next time I'm going to have to give you a ticket. Now you get you on home. I'm following you.*

"Uh-huh."

He walks over to his desk and dials the phone with his blunt forefinger. The rotor whirrs, and then the distant ringing in his ear.

"Maureen, yeah I know. Look, I know I told you I'd be home by three, but something's come up. Listen, I don't want none of your lip. It's business. That Welch girl. I can't talk about it here. I'll be home as soon as I can. No, this ain't something I want Dickey on. I know, I know, but I can't control what happens 'round here. I promise you I'll be home just as soon as I can. Goodbye."

Shaking his head, he gently places the phone back onto the receiver and heads back to the hat rack.

"Don't tell me you're leaving again. That phone's been ringing off the hook."

"I suspect it has," he says. "Look, I'm headed to stake out Bacons Bridge. Nothing dangerous, but it might take some intelligence, some delicacy, so I know you don't want me to assign either of them two clowns to it, do you?"

Inez laughs out loud. "You got a point there, Chief."

"If anything comes up, you can get me on the walkie-talkie."

As he walks out the door, Inez stubs Winston number 27 into the ashtray.

***

Even though the temperature has declined a degree from the day's high of 68, all three boys are sweaty after the ordeal of getting the USS Kerouac successfully secured on the boat trailer. At 11' x 8' it's wider than the trailer's designed for, but Eddie's a competent carpenter and mechanic, unlike Will, who at least can take directions and accomplish tasks, unlike poor AJ, who has the mechanical aptitude of an aardvark. Will is running back from the big house with some doomed red garment of Weeza's flapping like a pennant in his hands. Once at the trailer, he rips the red silk blouse in strips to provide Dorchester County motorists a sign that they're meeting up with a wide load, a long load, a dangerous load.

***

Ollie had checked his aviator watch when he first stepped into poolhall, and now he's hit the twenty-seven-minute mark. He's been here so long, trying to accomplish the quite un-heroic quest of procuring seven hot dogs, three all the way with onions, and four with just the patented chili. He feels as if he's failed. No telling how many have come after him only to be served before him, but finally, finally, his order is in. It might not be unreasonable for the girls have given up hope and abandoned him. Though, of course, ironically enough, that's irrational. Jill's not that type of girl. She wouldn't leave him here without a ride home any more than she'd come looking for him in a place like this. Despite the sign, he's heard plenty of profanity, weird-sounding elocutions like *what-you-gwine-do-bout-it-mo-fuckkah*. Oddly enough, though, the strange smell of the place, a mixture of smoke and some undeterminable sweet smell–pool chalk? …wall-mounted pyramids of talc? …bubbling chili? The strange smell of this place has sort of grown on him—he sort of likes it—though his eyes are starting to sting from the smoke.

The guy behind the bar—Buzz—he looks sort of like an owl with his brown-framed glasses and black turtleneck. This might be Ollie's order the owl-man is sliding carefully into a brown paper bag.

Behind him Bobbey Ray and Bucky Gaskin and Eddie Droze and Lonnie Bishop swagger outside. A domino trail of smiles follows them. Those in the know are glad to see them go.

Buzz notes their departure as he leans toward Ollie passing him the bag of hot dogs. "Keep it like this, bo," Buzz says, "flat like this so the chili doesn't drip."

"Thank you, Sir," Ollie says automatically, not dwelling on the poor service, merely happy to be on his long-delayed way. He's eager to return to the girls with these precious amalgams of various and sundry processed animal parts.

As he approaches the door, one of those boys in shop overalls holds the door open for him and follows him out.

"Thanks."

Outside, the sunlight stabs like it does after exiting an afternoon movie.

Ollie is looking up and down the sidewalk for the girls when someone grabs him from behind, pinning his arms behind him as the rude boy from the poolhall punches him in the stomach – ooooooommmmmppppp. Automatically, Ollie pulls his knees up, his feet off the sidewalk, and delivers a double kick straight to Bobbey Ray's diaphragm, and all 195 pounds of Bobbey Ray Bosheen crumples to the concrete. He's gasping for air as Ollie thrusts his feet downward flipping the surprisingly light assailant behind him over his shoulder onto Bobbey Ray. Unfortunately, Eddie Droze is right there and snatches Ollie's glasses from his head, flings them into the street, scratching Ollie's face in the process. Ollie spins, delivering a kick to Eddie's head, and he too collapses to the sidewalk, and here yet there's another one but he's backpedaling, backing up like he wants no part of Ollie.

Now Ollie's world is a blur. He didn't see or hear that car crunching his glasses; he doesn't know where the bag of hot dogs has gone, ruined anyway he suspects. Ollie's crouching, assuming the karate poses he's been practicing for years, never having had to put it to practical use, but hey, it seems to be working. Shapes are moving. Bucky has popped back up, and Bobbey Ray is tottering to his feet. "I'm gwine kill you, you sumbitch," he growls.

From the street a familiar voice. "Hey, Ollie, over here. C'mon, c'mon." It's Rusty Boykin; he's leaned over the seat and opened the back door so Ollie can rush in. Maintaining his crouch, slashing the empty air with threatening chops, Ollie maneuvers to the car and hops in. As soon as the door slams, Sandy floors the Mustang, leaving twin trails of tire tread on the asphalt and an impressive cloud of stinking burning rubber.

"Goddamn, Ollie," Rusty says, over the squeal and engine roar. "You're a regular James Bond. Where'd you learn that judo?"

"Karate," Ollie says. "It's karate."

"Man, oh man. It was like a movie or something. I've never seen anything like it. Sandy, you got any tissues? His face's bleeding."

"Look in the glove box," she says.

Rusty opens the glove *compartment*. There's no packet of tissues there. Only a vehicle registration, an insurance card, and photo of Tripp, smiling, holding a largemouth bass he's caught. *Dead, kaput, long gone, in the cold, cold ground. Missing out on all the fun. She must have left the scissors back at Will's.*

"Nope," Rusty says, "no luck."

"You mind dropping me off at the police station?" Ollie asks as Jill's Camaro, an undistinguishable beige blob, passes in the opposite direction.

"Well," Sandy says, "that might be a bit of a problem."

God, it's Sandy Welch. Ollie's not seen her since the accident. "Oh, hi, Sandy," he says, "I apologize for not greeting you, but I'm sort of frazzled."

"That's okay," Sandy says, her hair blowing back. "That was far out back there. Far out. You literally kicked some ass. Literally. Man, where did you learn that? Back in Minnesota?"

Rusty hates the cliché "far out," but, of course, he says nothing.

Ollie asks, "Why is going to the police a problem?"

"They're sorta of looking for us, 'rumor has it,'" Rusty says.

"Looking for whom? You and Sandy? Y'all? Whatever in the world for?"

"I dunno, Ollie," Rusty says. "I don't think we've done anything. I haven't. At least not today. Sandy, though, is a wild driver. Maybe a cop saw the car run a stop sign or something. I dunno."

Ollie touches the bridge of his nose, where his glasses should be. "Wouldn't it make more sense to go to the police and find out why they're looking for you? Trust me, if they want to find you, they'll find you, unless you plan on running away to Mexico."

Rusty laughs. "Now that's not a bad idea."

"No, it's a good idea," Ollie says.

"So, you think running away to Mexico is a good idea?" he says smiling.

***

The school is again quiet. The buses are lined up for the trip home, so Eula Lynne is headed to her brick veneer split-level to get to work on a retest. As she walks to the teacher's lot, stepping carefully in her heels, she sees her friend and colleague Frances Barrineau with that elegant leather briefcase of hers.

Fran's smiling. Obviously, she wasn't giving any tests. "My, oh my," Eula Lynne offers as a rueful greeting. "What a disastrous day."

"From what I've heard," Frances says, "things could have been a lot worse."

"I suppose," Eula Lynne admits, "I reckon it could have, though I do have half-taken tests sitting out there in the open. And the day started off with Alex Jensen mocking the devotional."

"That's unfortunate," Frances says, reaching in her purse for her keys as she approaches her gray late-model Oldsmobile 88. Suddenly, she looks over at Eula Lynne. *Poor Eula Lynne, that husband of hers. Some kind of a mechanic. That's what marrying your childhood sweetheart will get you.* You can see the idea take fire in her eyes. "You headed home?"

"I suppose I ought to start making out a new test."

"I have a better idea," Frances says.

"A better idea?"

"At least a more fun idea. Let's go to Guerrins and indulge ourselves by splitting a chocolate sundae. Then you can go make out that test. What's the hurry? This is a day we'll definitely remember when we're rocking on the porch of the retirement home. Let's end it with a bang, not a whimper, as the poet says. I read the other day—a depressing thought—obviously true, but I'd never considered it, that we have a finite number of sunsets left to enjoy."

Eula Lynne, who has never even taken a sip of wine, has a Smilodon-sized sweet tooth. She smiles. "Oh, I'd love to, but I really do have to get home and work on that test. But, I declare, a sundae sounds good."

"Indulge yourself," Frances suggests. "You could have burned up in a fire today. It was right on your hall."

"Right across from my room," Eula Lynne says.

***

Bacons Bridge is a Dorchester County landmark, crossing the tannic brown Ashley River some twenty miles northwest of Charleston. There's a dirt lane before the bridge that twists off to the right, down a rather steep descent to the river's edge. You wouldn't want to drive down there unless you had a Jeep. People do, though, park on the side of the road and walk down the lane. About twenty yards upriver stands a live oak carved with initials and names galore. There's a fat rope hanging from a limb. Tripp Trotter carved TT + SW in that tree just last August, the initials not yet blackened with time. In the summers, boys and girls take hold of the rope and run along the bank upstream, then swing out in a broad arc over the river, and at the zenith, let go, like Tarzans and Janes in cut-off blue jeans. Tripp used to do that. He had fond memories of this place. He loved this place.

John Bigelow has parked his unmarked Ford back at TC Limehouse's and walked through the woods to the river. He knows these woods. Shot a wild turkey two falls ago about fifty yards from this very spot. He knows that it's unlikely that the Welch girl is running away or committing suicide. She probably won't show up here. He prays she doesn't, but he'll make sure. He'll hide here at this vantage point until four or so and then go on home to face the wrath of Maureen. He's brought a book to read: *Survival… Zero,* the first Mike Hammer book out in three years.

Of course, real live detective work isn't glamorous. At least not in Summerville. The corpses you find around here are eighty-eight-year-old great grandmas in their housecoats, not these bosomy babes on the covers of paperback novels. Mostly, it's rough. That Trotter boy, stupid, impatient, impulsive. He's done gone and broke his mama's heart. His daddy's heart. His sister's heart. A waste. A goddamn waste.

***

In the school bus, headed to Boone Hill, Camilla looks out of the window as the colors flash by. Like a river. It can make you dizzy. This school bus she's riding in is, of course, newer and nicer than the one she lives in, but she's happy to go home and do her chores and to have her meal and to try to do some homework but most of all to close her eyes and imagine the fairy tale of her future.

***

Eddie, Will, and AJ have decided to put the raft in at Limehouse Landing, about three miles north of Bacon's Bridge. Eddie and AJ are riding together, while Will follows in the trailer-hitched new and improved bus. The plan is to put in and float down the river to Eddie's country house, and AJ can haul them back in his Beetle to retrieve their cars. Will has decided to spend the night with Eddie out in the country, leaving poor AJ with a dread-filled drive home to a *berserk-o mother*…or maybe, just maybe the disaster at school has short-circuited the calling tree. Who knows? Running away from home this very evening isn't in the cards. That's for sure. He wishes Rusty were here to talk some sense into Will.

205

Eddie's backing the truck down the ramp, and AJ and Will are on either side of it, pushing the raft into the water. It slides back afloat, secured by a line Eddie has tied to a piling. Eddie knows a lot about knots. No way AJ could have tied the raft down in the first place. He's never seen his ol' man pick up a tool. His ol' man pays other people to get his things done.

"Well, it floats," Eddie says. "I reckon it might float us three. I'll park the truck, and then we'll get going. This is one cool-looking floatation device. I'm not quite sure it qualifies as a boat. We'll see." He starts to sing, "way down upon the Sewanee River…"

AJ jumps on with his patented Paul Robertson Ol' Man River bass: "all the world is dark and dreary…"

***

Thud. Someone has rear-ended the Mustang. What else could go wrong?

Oh my God. It's them. The rednecks.

Wild looking. Rabid. One of them, the passenger – it's Bobbey Ray – has a hammer in his hand. The pick-up taps the Mustang's bumper again, so Sandy floors it, lurching Rusty and Ollie backward. Sandy's ripping through the gears, winding it out.

"Good God," Rusty says, "where did you learn to drive like this?"

"Jersey. The Shore," she says, glancing in the rearview at the truck that's falling behind.

"What do you think we ought to do?" Ollie asks.

"Lose these creeps," Sandy says.

Headed south up Main, Sandy takes a sudden left onto Gum Street, but the truck trails far back enough to make the left and then there's a stop sign, and they're t-boning into the school traffic at Spann Junior High, which has just let out. In a minor key Rusty whistles the equivalent of *bad move*. Sandy must slam on brakes and the truck is right behind her now, rocking back and forth, tapping her back bumper, like saying, come on, come on, I want a piece of y'all. The Mustang's doors have been long locked, but Rusty's worried that these goons are angry enough to smash the windshield with that hammer the bigger one in the passenger seat is menacingly waving back and forth. No, they wouldn't do that right here in a line of mamas picking up their seventh graders. The sidewalks are thick with kids walking home toward Twin Oaks and Rose Hill. But then again, Rusty's heard stories, the one about the gang fight at the Folly Beach Pier where one boy got thrown off and his neck broken. And then there was that time he and Vicki ran into a chain fight after last year's Homecoming game. Two throwbacks flailing one another with chains like gladiators in a Charlton Heston movie. But now—thank god—a blue Chevy is letting Sandy into the long line of cars so Bucky and Bobbey Ray will be at least one car behind.

They're headed southeast now, creeping toward another intersection to 165. This is a little less stressful. The road runs along a ditch that empties into the Tail Race Canal. The shop boys are now three cars behind but blowing their horns like maniacs. Oh no, one car is easing over to let them by. This is some deep completely random shit they've wandered into. On the plus side, Rusty's worries about the Anatomy test and incipient fatherhood have been shoved off the table onto the floor (along with his fears of permanent acne scarring and likelihood of a nuclear exchange with the USSR).

***

After they found a parking place and waited ten minutes, Jill and the girls conducted a mini conference on what to do. They, of course, don't know Ollie well. A shy, good-looking boy being that smart, it's sort of scary. Like he is an adult or something. Too grown up in the mind, not very playful, but sincere, honest, modest. The last person to enact a cruel practical joke, to leave them in the lurch. But what to do? Three virgins, all three the younger daughter of a doting prosperous father, all members of the Christian organization Young Life, sitting in a parked car right outside the notorious poolhall, thinking about going inside, breaking a serious taboo, ruining their reputations. You could count the number of females who had ever entered the poolhall on your left hand. A brazen hussy, a runaway, and Buzz's mother. But what else is there to do? Going in and inquiring about Ollie's whereabouts is the most reasonable option. Surely, anyone would understand. It's sort of like a husband going into a beauty parlor to ask for his wife during an emergency. The women wouldn't like it necessarily, but they would understand if it were an emergency. Kathi says it's ridiculous that they're so hesitant to do it. In fact, she's been contemplating wearing a pantsuit on a Friday, a non-pants day, just to see what happens. "Hell, if y'all don't go. I'll go by myself. It's not like I'm going in there to see if I can pick me up a shop boy."

"Let's do it," Nanci says. "I'm just about famished."

"Okay," Jill says.

As they exit the Camaro and tiptoe toward the door, Kathi says, "This is sort of exciting. I've often wondered what it's like in there. I guarantee you it's going to be disappointing. No big deal."

Hesitantly, Kathi opens the door to smelly, smoky, loud. Conversations are halting, though, the decibel level diminishing, so now you can hear the jukebox playing "Bad Moon Rising."

"Well, looky, there," a bass voice cooingly says, "Well, I'll be damned. Well, hell-loooooooo, Ladies."

Ignoring the voice, with Ollie nowhere in sight, Kathi and the girls timidly approach the near end of the bar where the blind man sits with his dog. As soon as Buzz spots them, he drops the deep fryer back into the bubbling grease and walks hurriedly to the girls, rubbing his hands on the towel that dangles from his belt.

"Hey," he says in an unfriendly voice. "What y'all doing in here?"

"A friend of ours came in here a while ago," Kathi says, "almost forty minutes ago, to order some hot dogs for us, but we can't find him. We were circling the block looking for a parking place, but now we can't find him."

"What did he look like?"

"Sorta tall. Parts his hair in the middle. Wears granny glasses."

"Yeah," Buzz says, "he left here about twenty or thirty minutes ago."

"Thanks," the girls say and head hurriedly to the door. The military man banging a pinball machine glares at them as they leave. An unpleasant spinal rush sends a shiver through Jill.

***

At the intersection of 165, traffic's heavy. There's still a car between Sandy and the goons. It's an Electra 225, a dark green Deuce-and-a-Quarter, driven by some sharp older Black dude sporting a gray felt fedora with an exotic feather in its band. His head is in the middle of the car, his left arm draped over the steering wheel, but Rusty sees now that the head's looking to the left, right, and center rear view mirrors, nervously trying to figure out what's going on with all the impatient honking.

There's a deep dark fear down in his belly, but Catman ain't letting these crackers get past him to do what badness they hell-bent on committing. They're giving him the finger, hollering racial epithets, but he's playing deaf, shuffling nervously in the seat, easing over to the shoulder to block them *Goddamn cracker ass crackers.*

Beowulf. Wergild. Grendel. Apeshit. Tarzan of the Apes. Conan the Barbarian. Bullshit. Muscle-bound testosteronic holograms of wannabe. These fellows – these so-called *citizens—chasing us—they're berserk, angry. We're gonna die. Not gonna, might gonna. Likely gonna. Look on the bright side. Maybe merely permanent disfigurement, a chewed off ear and/or bitten off nose. Rusty, Phantom of the Rock Opera.*

At the stop sign at 165, Sandy times her rubber-burning, fishtailing left a split second before what would be a collision with on-coming traffic. Brakes behind her squeal. Laughing out loud, she figures she's trapped the rednecks behind the braking cars, blocking them like offensive lineman, while she and the boys screech off toward Bacons Bridge Road to paydirt.

Nope, the rednecks spin tires, too, ripping into traffic, passing three cars by swerving right on the shoulder, then the fourth in the left lane, and now they're right behind Sandy, streaking past Sweat's Grocery.

"Look, y'all," Ollie says, "this may sound counterintuitive, but I'd be willing to bet that if you, Sandy, continue to make even unremarkable evasive moves, that these overreactive idiots behind us are quite likely to lose control of their truck. The less populated the intersection, the better. In fact, the lower center of gravity of your vehicle gives us an advantage. You should be able to cut corners at a greater speed. They're likely to roll that truck if they're not careful."

"No, careful is not what I'd call them," Rusty says.

"I ought to be able to outrun that truck once I get out on 61 where I can wind it out and be out of their sight when I make my turn."

"Okay, if you think so," Ollie says. "You certainly seem to know what you're doing."

To Sandy, none of this much matters. Driving fast feels good. These rednecks can't catch her.

But now there's traffic to contend with, a tractor lurching along at 25 in a 40-mph zone, past the Church of the Nazarene. An on-coming cement truck rolls past, and, once again, the pickup's right behind them.

"You don't happen to have those scissors on you?" Rusty asks, half-kidding, trying to sound brave.

Sandy's easing up on the gas.

"Why are you slowing down?" Ollie asks.

"Oh my god," Sandy says.

"Oh my god what? I was only kidding about the scissors."

"It's started. Oh my god. It's started."

"What's started? Look, we're almost already at Bacons Bridge. There's only one more stop sign ahead after that. Maybe after that, you can shake them. Why are you slowing down?"

"Prepare for bat turn," Sandy says. Suddenly, she slams on brakes and jerks the wheel to the left, the Mustang sliding into a u-turn, banging into the rail of the bridge, bouncing off the rail, spinning. By the time the Mustang comes to a stop on the shoulder of the road past the bridge, the rednecks have disappeared, but then there's the awful sound of crunching metal and exploding glass.

***

It's peaceful on the river, and the raft handles just fine with that keel John D. John rigged up. The brown water is as smooth as glass, the shadows have lengthened, and golden sunlight strobes through the leaves of live oaks dripping with moss. The three boys smiling, having fun, the

Bacons Bridge Bend ahead, the scene of Tripp's deadly accident that each one thinks of quietly and separately, and as they round that bend, they see something that none of them will ever forget as long as they live: a pickup truck caroming down the river embankment and splashing down into the water with an enormous whhhhooooooooooshhhhhh.

"Jesus Christ!" Eddie shouts as he steers the raft away from the wake.

Miraculously, two figures are out of the truck floating with the current, the truck now sinking, one boy moaning like a wounded elephant. Eddie guides the raft back to the left as Will extends an oar to the big one and AJ to the little one.

"Anyone else in the truck?" Eddie screams. "Anyone else in the truck!"

The little one's shaking his head no, so they struggle to pull them aboard, but can't, so Eddie maneuvers the raft to the river's edge with them hanging on to the side.

The fat one is whimpering. AJ winces because he thinks he might see a bone sticking out of the arm. He hopes they're no sharks in these waters.

"Of all the Goddamn luck," Eddie says. "You know who this one with the broken arm is?"

"Who is it?" Will asks.

"Bobbey Ray Bosheen," Eddie says. "Of all the Goddamned luck. We've gone and saved Bobbey Ray Bosheen's life. We'll never live this down. We'll never be forgiven for this. Damn it. It's always been a fantasy of mine to save a life, and now I've gone and done so, but it's Bobbey Ray Bosheen's life I've saved."

"Sort of like giving mouth-to-mouth to Hitler?" AJ cracks.

"Of all the goddamn luck."

"Speaking of luck," Will says, "but isn't that Big John Bigelow that's yelling back there."

"How in the hell did he get here? Jesus Christ. Well, if there's ever a time you might not mind seeing a cop, this is it. Hand me that rope, AJ. I'm gonna tie this to that stump. Let's see if we can get them on their feet. Of all the Goddamned luck. Bobbey Ray Bosheen. I'll never be able to show my face in the poolhall again."

***

Jill's stepmother Dee was not happy with Jill when she got home after four without having called to let her know what was up. After all, everyone in town had heard about the accident at school, but Jill was quick to relate a somewhat sanitized version of the story (omitting the poolhall entrance, for example), and Dee immediately instructed Jill to call Ollie's house to see if he was all right, so she looked up Wyborn in the phone book—there was only one Wyborn—and punched in the numbers on her Princess phone.

"Hello, Wyborn house. Mrs. Wyborn speaking."

"Hello, Mrs. Wyborn. This is Jill Birdsong, one of Ollie's friends from school. Could I speak with Ollie, please?"

"Why, dear. He's not home yet. I don't know where in the world he is. Maybe the bus broke down."

"Oh no."

"Oh no? What's the matter?"

"Mrs. Wyborn. Ollie didn't ride the bus. I was giving him a ride home from school. Didn't you hear that school was let out early?"

"Let out early?"

"Yes, Ma'am. There was an accident in the chemistry lab. Nobody was hurt, but they had to let everybody go because of the fumes. Anyway, we stopped to pick up some fast food, and we couldn't find a parking space, so Ollie hopped out, and he's sort of disappeared."

"Disappeared! Oh my God!"

"I'm sorry, Mrs. Wyborn. I hate to worry you, but I thought you needed to know."

"What did you say your name was again?"

"Jill Birdsong."

"Thank you, Jill. I need to hang up now. I'm going to call the police."

***

It took the ambulance seventeen plus minutes to arrive at the scene. Bobbey Ray indeed had broken his arm, and Bucky suffered contusions and cuts on his face and arms from jagged glass shards encountered as he climbed through the windshield onto the hood of the sinking truck. Now, he's lying on a stretcher that's being lifted and placed next to Bobbey Ray, who after an injection is out cold.

Sandy's Mustang is worse for the wear as well, the right-hand side bashed in from its collision with the guardrail, its rear end dented from the frequent smacks it received from Bucky's truck. Officer Dickey has arrived, so

John Bigelow has called him over to see the ambulance off. Having already taken Sandy's keys so she can't go anywhere, Big John climbs wearily up the embankment to deal again with her and the boys. He knows the Old Summerville Boykin boy, and likely he's a good boy. At least his brother David is. This Sandy, though, looks like bad news, and he's never heard of the Wyborn boy, but what he's saying sounds about right, except for the karate bit, which is hard for John Bigelow to imagine. Of course, John has had dealings with Bobbey Ray's daddy, a hardened case if there ever was one. There are no social services down here to speak of. Throw one of these jokers in jail for domestic abuse, and the chillen end up going hungry. They just take it out on the poor women when they get out of jail, fifty dollars poorer.

"I would like to press charges," Ollie's saying. "You know, assault and battery. They broke my glasses."

Down at the raft, Eddie, AJ, and Will have been told to sit tight. Will's stash is long gone, floating down the river toward the Atlantic Ocean. There wasn't much of it anyway. They're getting their stories straight in case Big John asks them about the raft. They decide to say that John D. John built it for them, that they paid him, which is sort of true, in a way. Eddie still can't believe he's gone and saved Bobbey Ray Bosheen's life.

Sandy's period has definitely started, so she asks the older policeman if she can ask him something in private. He looks suspicious, but she can't be that good of an actress feigning embarrassment, so he lets her get her purse and directs her around behind some bushes. He can't imagine her running away through the woods, and she doesn't seem a bit suicidal to him. What's that cliché? A little knowledge is a dangerous thing. Ought to keep those school counselors like Josie Palmer away from psychology courses. Ought to keep everybody away from them as far as he's concerned. Dr. Spock. Look what it's got us. Then again, he suspects that Bobbey Ray's old man wasn't exactly the permissive type and look at him.

***

Down by the raft, Eddie's saying, "I don't see why we're being held here. I know rescuing Bobbey Ray is probably wrong, but it can't be against the law."

Will says, "Maybe he wants to give us a medal or something. I can see the headline in the *Scene/Journal*:

High School Drop Out Saves Students' Lives

"Yeah right," AJ says.

Eddie looks down the river, shielding his eyes. "I got a good mind to slip this rope off and continue our little escapade," he says.

AJ's frowning. "I dunno. I got to be getting home."

"Home?" Will says.

"With school getting out early and all. Maybe they didn't get around to calling Mama, maybe they've forgotten about everything, and I can go back to school tomorrow like nothing's happened."

"I knew you'd wuss out," Will says.

"You just can't go freelancing like this. Changing the timeframe from summer to fall."

"What's he talking about?" Eddie asks.

"I'll tell you later, Eddie," Will says and turns to AJ.

"But, hey, if you split, how are we going to go fetch my bus and Eddie's truck?"

"Here are the keys," AJ says, tossing them to Will. "Drop the car by the house sometime tomorrow. I'll get Mama to give me a ride to school."

***

Sandy's back now, wearing a beatific smile. Smashed car worries are nothing compared to unwanted pregnancy via dead daddy worries. Both Rusty and Ollie ask for "bathroom" turns, and each beats a path behind the bushes Sandy used. As they're finishing up, jingling droplets onto pine straw, Rusty says, "Man, I still can't believe those karate moves you laid on those cats. Wish I could do that. Is it hard?"

"I could show you a couple of the basic moves. A lot of it is about concentration and harnessing your opponent's energy to work against him."

"No kidding? Hey, changing the subject, did y'all finish *Macbeth* today?"

"Yep. It's over. Mrs. Barrineau recited that famous 'tomorrow and tomorrow' speech by heart."

"It is a tale told by an idiot—full of sound and fury— signifying nothing."

"You really have a good memory, don't you?" Ollie says.

"Yeah. But I'm careless and lazy. That's what everybody—all my teachers—say."

218

"Hey, Ollie, you're a smart guy; I'd say the smartest guy in the whole school."

"I don't know about that."

"Well, I say you are. There's been a question that has been bugging me my whole life, especially today. And it came up earlier, and I think it might have been answered today, but I want to see what you think. Okay?"

"Sure."

"Anyway, do you believe in God? Sandy asked me that earlier today, and I said no, but now I really don't know. If you look at today, for example, it seems like things might be happening for a reason. I get kicked out of school because it just happens to be AJ's turn to read the devotional, then get picked up hitchhiking by Sandy, who I've been thinking about a lot all week because of Tripp and all, and Sandy just happens to see me at that particular moment. Then we just happen to be at the poolhall because a dog we were responsible for just happened to run away, and you're attacked. And then, even more unbelievably, just when those goons crash their truck into the river, Will and them come floating up at the exact second like the cavalry. It's too unbelievable to be true."

"Or it's coincidence," Ollie says. "Look, somewhere else on this planet while these idiots are being coincidentally saved some other idiot is running a stop sign and killing someone innocent who wouldn't be there at that exact second to die if he had only gone upstairs to turn off that light he'd left on. In fact, I was in the poolhall getting hot dogs for Jill Birdsong and Kathi Haley and Nanci Boyd, and there's no telling what they think has happened. But to answer your question, I guess you could say I don't believe in an anthropomorphic god, a god in man's image."

Bigelow (shouting): What in the hell are you boys doing back there?

***

Back beyond at the bridge, traffic is crawling as rubberneckers try to assess what's happened. Big John explains to Sandy that her parents have been called and that her father is on the way to pick her up. Even though her car still runs, a wrecker has been summoned to take it to Weber's Body Shop. Throughout the explanation, she just stands there smiling stupidly.

"You sure you didn't get a bump on the head?" Bigelow asks.

"Oh, no sir. I'm fine."

Just then AJ walks up. "Hello, sir," he says to Bigelow, "Eddie and Will have left, because they're in a hurry, but they've sent me here to explain. Hey, Rusty. Ollie."

Bigelow seems uninterested. "Fine, fine," he says.

***

Finally, Mr. Welch arrives, a tall, good-looking man with thick, salt-and-pepper hair and a coat and tie. Bigelow explains to him what happened, and Rusty can see palpable signs of relief as Mr. Welch's body sort of relaxes, loses its stiffness. It's not her fault, even if these characters she's with don't look all that savory. And she seems to have forgotten that Rusty exists. He keeps looking to her for signs of love, or at least, recognition, but none are forthcoming. "Bye, you guys," is all she says as she waves, turns, and gets into her father's Mercedes, disappearing slowly in the distance as the Mercedes bends out of sight. Rusty can't believe it. He feels abandoned. Crushed. Lost. And he knows it. It's over even before it started. His body can feel it. Emptiness spreads through him like a stain. Then he remembers his bookbag's in Sandy's car and retrieves it from the back seat.

"Well, boys," Bigelow says. "As soon as this wrecker's out of here, I'll give you a ride downtown. Bet you've never ridden in a police car, not yet anyways."

As the wrecker's flashing lights blink on-and-off headed for Summerville, Rusty and AJ gravitate toward the back seats, leaving Ollie to sit in the front, which he is probably best equipped to do.

"Well, well, well," Bigelow says. "This has been one hell of a week."

"One hell of a day," Ollie says, and AJ and Rusty do twin double takes in the back seat.

"You grow up fast in these here parts," AJ says in his pretty good John Wayne accent, which produces a surprised glance from Bigelow in the rearview mirror.

"Look, Ollie, about those charges you want to file. What if I had a long talk with Bobbey Ray about joining the Marines instead of going to jail? Jail's not going to do him any good. The Marines might. He can channel that hatred in, um, more positive ways."

"I see. Well, I'll need to talk to my father."

"Please, do. Have him give me a call. By the way, gentlemen, where would you like to be let off, at the poolhall?"

"No thanks," Ollie says. "As a matter of fact, I live just up here in Twin Oaks. You can just let me out at the gas station up here, and I'll walk home."

Ollie had enough of the poolhall for one day. Anyway, according to his calculations, he could make it home from here in about twelve to fourteen minutes, and driving downtown, calling his parents to pick him up, then returning home would be a thirty-five to forty-minute endeavor at best. There's a pay phone at the gas station.

"Oh, no, I'm sure your friends wouldn't mind if I took you all the way home after what you've been through."

"To tell you the truth, sir. I'd rather be let out here. I need to make a phone call, and I'd like to walk home, to be able to gather my thoughts in silence, as it were, before I go home."

Bigelow puts on his left turn signal and pulls into the station. There's a fat woman in a glass booth to take the motorists' money. The sun's starting to set, and traffic from the Air Force Base and Navy Yard is starting to stack up on Trolley Road.

"Okay, Ollie. Here you go. Have that talk with your daddy and have him call me, okay? We can take care of those glasses for you."

"Yes, sir."

***

222

On the way home Mr. Welch tells Sandy that he and her mother have made an important decision, that they're moving back to New York, and Sandy's docility at receiving the news surprises him. He could imagine either extreme—ecstatic joy or banshee keening. Mr. Welch—Dave—stresses to Sandy her mother's unhappiness here and the exciting business opportunity he has in New York. They'll be able to go see the Macy's Thanksgiving Day Parade again, the Rockettes, the plays. He is, in fact, employing the mirror image of Sandy's argument when she was told they were moving to sub-tropical South Carolina.

"You don't seem too excited," Dave says.

"I sort of have mixed emotions."

"I can understand that."

"But, you know, this place seems sort of unlucky, if you know what I mean."

Dave smiles ruefully. "Yes, I do. I know what you mean."

"I just wish people would leave me alone. Let me be."

"Why do you say that?"

"It's like people like me too easy or too much and then want me all to themselves. I don't know, Dad. I don't know. I just wish people would leave me alone."

***

Dee Birdsong herself is concerned with Ollie's disappearance but sitting around worrying isn't going to do anybody any good.

Half-heartedly doing her chores, Jill has chosen to dust the foyer first because of its proximity to a phone that offers some privacy, but then she's called into the kitchen to peel potatoes, a rare treat in these rice-eating parts. There's a fancy, sleek avocado push-button phone mounted on the wall, and when it rings, Jill drops her knife on the counter and rushes to answer it.

"Hello, this is Ollie Wyborn. May I speak to Jill please?"

"Oh my God, Ollie. Where have you been?"

"Jill? Hey, Jill, I'm so, so sorry. It's a long story. I was robbed outside the poolhall. Jumped, beaten up, sort of. Involved in a high-speed car chase. I'll tell you all about it, but I need to ask you something first."

Jill is confused, overwhelmed. "Okay?"

"Jill, will you go to the Homecoming Dance with me? Oh, yeah, and the game, too."

"Well, I'm on the drill team, so I can't sit with you at the game, but I'd love to go to the dance with you."

"Oh man, that's great. Thank you!"

"Ollie, what's that noise?"

"A truck blowing its horn."

"You're not home?"

"No, I'm at a pay phone."

"Have you been home yet?"

"No, not yet."

"You have talked to your mother, though?"

"No, not yet."

"Oh, you need to hang up and call her. She's worried sick about you. But call me right back, okay? I mean, as soon as you can."

"Of course, of course."

"Okay, bye bye. I'll talk to you later."

"I promise I'll call. Goodbye."

After Ollie races across Trolley Road and cuts through Rose Hill to his subdivision Twin Oaks, he stops to jump up, and he clicks his heels twice, waves of something electrically weird going on deep down under the epidermis. Then he breaks into a run, headed home, eager to call Jill to tell her all about what happened. Wow, what a weird, weird, wonderful day.

***

Instead of quizzing the boys about the raft and its ill-gotten lumber, Bigelow is asking them questions about what they think of policemen.

"I bet you hate them," he says indifferently, as if he's not one of "them."

"Well," Rusty says, "not all cops. We certainly don't hate you, Mr. Bigelow. In fact, I think you're pretty cool, if you don't mind my saying so."

What an asslick, AJ thinks.

"So you wouldn't call me a pig behind my back?"

"I wouldn't. Some might. Most people I know call you Big John."

"What about Dickey?" Bigelow asks. "Would you call him a pig behind his back?"

"No sir," Rusty says, "I wouldn't call any policeman a pig. I call y'all cops."

"So, you don't hate Dickey?"

"Hate's not the right word," Rusty says. "I see him as a sort of necessary evil. If you got maniacs like Bobbey Ray running around, I suspect you need some mean cops. Only, it's hard telling sometimes who's worse, or rather, it's not like there's much difference between the two. I mean between rednecks and cops. No offense, sir."

"None taken," Bigelow says and is quiet, his uncharacteristic chattiness at an end.

"Hey, Rusty," AJ says to Rusty after eons of awkward silence. "Neither of your parents is home from work yet, are they?"

"No."

"Why don't you come home with me?"

"I dunno."

"Please, man. You can explain why I got kicked out of school today."

"You didn't exactly get kicked out. I got kicked out. You cut."

Bigelow glances in the rearview mirror but doesn't say anything.

"C'mon, man. I'm practically begging."

"All right already," Rusty says. "It doesn't matter. I've sort of lost the will to live anyway."

"No, not fast enough," Bigelow says.

"I'm sorry, sir. What?"

"You know, you don't grow up *fast* in these parts. You grow up *slow*. In Nam, that's where you grow up fast. Or on Normandy Beach. If I was you boys, I'd cut my hair, try to blend in, do my goddamned homework, so I could go off to college and get out of this place. High school ain't about freedom. It's about whipping your ass into shape. Save your freedom-seeking for college. They cotton to it more up there."

Out on the river, away from the blare of truck horns and the flashing lights of tow trucks and ambulances, it's downright peaceful. The sun is now below the tree lines, and in the dry air of the high-pressure system overhead, the light is pure, golden, almost like the light in that Maxfield Parrish poster in Rusty's room. Will has broken down and told Eddie the complete story of the BSO, and Eddie cannot believe how stupid the idea is.

"Man, that's crazy. Immature. It's like you can't tell the difference between a book and real life. It's dangerous out there, like this little incident with these hillbillies today. Hey man, I got a better idea."

"Better than what?"

"Better than abandoning this raft in the river, running to try to catch a freight train, most likely getting crushed under its steel wheels in the attempt or breaking your neck trying to jump out. Or getting arrested and spending the night in jail with a bunch of drunken sodomites."

"But what could be better than that?" Will jokes.

"Going to Europe."

"Europe?"

"Yeah, Europe. I've already applied for a passport. You apply for one, too. We can bum around Europe for a while together. I'm going, no matter what. But it would be less lonesome with you, cousin. Those other friends of yours, AJ and Rusty, they're still just a couple of little boys."

"Think about it. You and me can talk Weeza into anything. Promise her you'll get your G.E.D. as soon as you get back. That's what I told my folks. I'd go back and get my degree when I got back. Going to Europe would be a much more valuable education than sitting around memorizing the dates of long-ago battles fought in the Middle Ages out of some GED prep book."

"Man, Eddie. You're singing my song. That's so cool. Hell, those guys would never go through with the BSO anyway."

"That's cause deep down inside they know it's all bullshit."

"Europe! Let's make a pact right here. On this raft. Let's swear. Make up the oath, and I'll swear."

"See, that's what I'm talking about," Eddie says. "That's kids' stuff. Just give me your word."

"You got it."

For a minute or two, they drift down river in silence, the golden light diminishing with encroaching darkness.

Looking at the trail of water behind the raft, Will says, "Today, oh boy. What a day. I sort of wish it wouldn't end."

"You mean, like your childhood?" Eddie asks. "Well, mine's over, and yours is on its last legs."

"Yeah," Will says, "I know, and I'm betting adulthood isn't what it's all cracked up to be."

"Well, let's focus on the positive. I got a case of Old Mill back at the house."

The raft drifts over to the left bank, Will ducks beneath a branch, picks up an oar, pushes off, and looks back at the raft's insignificant wake.

"If Rusty were here, he'd be singing 'Ol' Man River.' I'm gonna miss Rusty. You know, he's always quoting passages from books. Shit that makes you think. One of his favorites is – he says it so often even I've memorized it."

"Well, what is it?"

"Nobody, nobody knows what's going to happen to anybody besides the forlorn rags of growing old."

Eddie shakes his head in disapproval. "Like I said, let's focus on the positive. I got a case of Old Mill in the fridge."